THE AMERADA AFFAIR

A mystery novel

By

ALAN WALLACH

<u>O</u>ther Works By The Author

The Kieran Adventure Series for Young Readers

Book 1 Kieran and the Weird Window

Book 2 Kieran and the Visitor from Pimglammam

Book 3 Kieran and Rajilad's Time Warp

Book 4 Kieran and the Robots.

Moffett's Wife

Corviglia, An Alpine Murder Mystery

Solomon's Dozen-Escapades of a Dirty Old Man

The Super

A Long Drunk and a Breakfast

The Year 2000 Hoax

Published by
Interlaken Publishing Co.
5 Tenafly Rd. Box 106
Englewood, NJ 07631

Distributed by amazon.com
ISBN 978-0-9965080-9-4

website: alanwallach.com
email:alanwallach@gmail.com

CHAPTER I

Dr. Barnhill's Office

The hour was late but Dr. Hugo Barnhill of HB Security Agency was curious enough to stay in his office a while longer. Dr. Barnhill was an impatient man. He was never prone to leave things for tomorrow. The fluorescent lighting over his desk bothered him so he always turned it off before sitting at his computer. The room was not totally dark, but was dimly lit from the hall light and the glow from his computer screen saver. He sat down, put on his glasses and rubbed his hands together as if to warm them, a superstitious ritual he did for years before he put his hands on the keyboard or his mouse.

He had been trying to access an NSA account called Amerada at the request of Sarah Tepper for two days without any progress. Barnhill knew there had been two murders in the last two weeks, both involving this seemingly innocuous National Security Agency account that nobody at NSA admitted to owning. Anxious as he was to get started, he decided to check his email before he started his concentrated energy attack on the account. He had no family and although he wasn't lonely, he was always afraid to miss something.

As he dragged his mouse down the list of emails, he laughed. Dr. Barnhill was a fiftyish balding nerd who mumbled to himself, "Why do they always send me these sex solicitations?" He read aloud to himself, "Veronica lives in your neighborhood and wants to meet you." He clicked on the "yes" button and a voluptuous brown-haired beauty started talking. "Would you like to chat for a while to see if we want to get together?" He shook his head and clicked on the "no" button, which for some reason initiated an unusually loud computer hum. "This damn computer is always doing something." He thought it must be the computer's internal fan, which always bothered him, so he forced himself to ignore it.

He went to the Amerada screen and using special software he designed, hoped to break into the account this time. The first time it failed. He tried again using another option to explore further and he was still denied access. "Shit," he mumbled. "Why in hell is this?" he thought to himself, "Is this project so classified?" It wasn't supposed to be and besides, I've been authorized. He pushed the mouse around some more and stopped, putting his hand under his goatee in a thinking pose. The computer hum continued to grow louder to the point where he couldn't ignore it. He picked up the telephone to call his hardware serviceman's cell phone, but before he was finished keying in the phone number, he was blown back away from his exploding computer screen. He probably never heard the loud blast that killed him instantly.

One Hour Later

Detectives Randy Chekhov and Elena LoPlana looked at the mutilated, bloody face of Hugo Barnhill. LoPlana took photographs and marked the outline of the body in chalk before the EMT men had lifted the body to a gurney and into a plastic zipper bag. Chekhov, at 6'3", towering over the diminutive security guard, asked him what happened. Chekhov stifled a yawn as if bored by the whole thing. He was jaded and it showed. The guard told them that he heard a monster blast and this is what he found.

"Was anyone else in the building?" Chekhov asked calmly.

"I don't know" the guard stuttered nervously, obviously in shock over the whole thing. I came on shift at four and everyone was starting to leave the building. I didn't see anyone come in tonight but there might have been others that didn't leave, I don't know." Then he added, "Although, I gotta say that there aren't usually any stragglers in the other offices. Everyone that I know of always leaves before 5:30."

"Did anyone have access to Barnhill's office?"

He shook his head."I wouldn't know. There is a key in the lock box downstairs in case of emergency. But when I heard the explosion, I looked to get the keys in case I needed them and found the box still locked. I would guess that no one in the building even gives a shit about Barnhill. He kept pretty much to himself."

Randy looked at his partner. Elena was a zaftig dark-haired woman, and despite some extra weight, she was attractive and curvy. He said with some expression in his voice, "How the fuck did someone plant a bomb in the computer? It doesn't look like a new one." He looked at the remnants strewn all over the floor. "Leni, call the precinct and get someone from forensics in here. I don't even know where to start." He picked up the agenda that was on the floor several feet away from Barnhill's body and started to browse through it. The last entry was NSA with a phone number written and the word 'Amerada.' He dialed the number but there was no answer and no message. He looked at his watch. Better to call in the morning, he thought. He took the agenda and put it in his pocket. He would try to find out what Barnhill was working on. Maybe it would give him an idea where to start.

Elena dialed the precinct and waited. The voicemail referred to a cell phone number in case of an emergency which Elena dialed. "Tony? Elena LoPlana. Can you come over to 660 E.48th Street, 2nd floor? We've got a weird situation." Elena explained what they could see and the puzzling nature of the blast.

"Sounds interesting," Tony said. "I'll be there in a half hour. Don't touch anything. Just wait for me."

"Sorry, the EMT guys took the body. I took good pictures."

"OK. Wait for me and leave things as they are." The two detectives continued browsing around with not the slightest idea what they were looking for.

"Where the hell is he?" Chekhov asked, impatiently just as Antonio Belvedere stepped into the office looking back at the broken door window. He put down his back pack, looked around at the remnants of the computer.

"Holy shit," he said as he put his hand out to shake the detectives hands. "I've never seen anything like this. This computer isn't massive enough to hold a bomb big enough to kill like that. It's pretty thin. Back in the day, computers were heavy and bulky. It would make sense. But most of these new computers are built skinny with thin high definition screens. You say it apparently blew up and killed this guy, what's his name, Barnhill?"

"That seems to be what happened," LoPlana answered. "As best we can figure."

Belvedere was in his late thirties, with rugged good looks, stocky build and with thick salt and pepper gray hair that had a small white streak running through it in front. He was the police forensic expert and was especially computer literate. His Italian accent was almost imperceptible but Elena could hear it. He looked at the computer carefully as well as the pieces scattered around the floor. "I'd like to take this stuff to my lab. I'll inventory it and send you a report. Maybe I can figure out what happened."

"Great but I need you to sign an evidence receipt that I can file with my report. The captain is a fucking stickler for paperwork."

Belvedere zipped open his back pack and pulled out a pad of evidence receipts and wrote one out, dated and signed it. Chekhov took the receipt and stuffed it in his pocket. He took Barnhill's agenda from his pocket and handed it to Belvedere. "Tell me if you find anything useful in this. I found it on the floor near the computer remnants. I called the number in the note for today but no answer."

Belvedere grabbed a black heavy-duty plastic bag from his back pack and began collecting the scattered pieces of the exploded computer, lingering a little on every piece before putting it in the bag. When all the pieces were gathered, he closed the black bag and said. "I think I've got everything."

"Let us know what you find." Chekhov added, still appearing to be only marginally interested. "This is the third death in the last two weeks. The other two seemed to be associated with an NSA project. At least one was. The other was his girlfriend but didn't seem to be a coincidence. As long as they're not related to this one, the case is ours. But if this one is related to the other two, that is, to an NSA project, we'll have to turn it over to the feds."

"I'll let you know as soon as I find out anything. Take care." He left, loaded down with his back pack, the black bag of pieces and the solid intact piece of the computer under his arm.

When Belvedere got out of the taxi and went into his lab, the building was empty except for the security guard. He put everything down and decided not to do anything until morning. As he left to go to the subway, he thought a car that had been outside the building was following him but pushed it out of his mind as he walked down the subway steps to take the #6 train uptown to 86th Street. Paranoia I don't need now, he mumbled to himself.

NSA Office of Sarah Tepper

Sarah Tepper had been with NSA for twelve years, since she got her masters degree. There was no NSA glamor for her as with some others. She was the office administrative manager and served the office needs of several sections. It was a desk job and routine for her had become routine. She never envied the operatives whom she felt were always endangering themselves. But these last few days, she had been poring over the reports furnished to her by the NewYork City police regarding the deaths of Paul Conaghey and his girlfriend Margaret Casey the next day. He was a hit and run accident and left alongside the West Side Highway. She was mugged outside the hotel they were staying at and strangled.

Conaghey was an independent operative on an NSA assignment working on something in New York City but Sarah couldn't find out what, or who at NSA was employing his services. She had no idea what he was doing in New York and no one in the agency would admit to knowing. It was the first time at NSA she was in any way involved in cloak and dagger stuff. She didn't like it and wanted it settled as soon as possible. It destroyed her comfortable routine. She had no idea how or if Ms. Casey was involved but her death the next day was a coincidence too strange to ignore.

Sarah was tall, 5'7", lithe with an athletic body and dark blond shoulder-length kinky-curly hair, parted on the left. She was at the window thinking as she watched the people passing below. As best she could ascertain, Conaghey was involved in an account named Amerada, about which Sarah did not have the slightest information, nor could she find out who he was working for. His girlfriend was apparently not involved in any way except that she was his girlfriend.

When the NYPD told Sarah about the deaths and something called Amerada which was on a piece of paper in Conaghey's pocket, Sarah looked for and found the Amerada account. She tried for several days to get into it but was denied access, unusual because she had the requisite security clearance and was authorized with a "need to know." Strange as that was, even more puzzling was that she couldn't find out who the administrator was, the one who could block access to the account. She asked around and then addressed a formal email to the section heads and their respective tech-ops officers. Responses indicated that no one seemed to know who was in charge of the account. More confusing still was that no one with appropriate authority was able to unblock the account. In fact, no one knew anything about the Amerada project. There was no one in charge of it that she could find. She was frustrated because she didn't know and couldn't find out who assigned Paul Conaghey to the project and what his assignment was. Maybe he was taking it on himself, she thought. He was an experienced operative.

She had decided to enlist the services of Hugo Barnhill, who had helped her once before when she felt she couldn't trust anyone in-house. She had talked to him the day before yesterday to see if he could find anything out. Anxious to know how he was doing, she dialed his number and was surprised when there was no answer on his phone She would try again later.

When her phone started ringing soon after, Sarah picked up hoping it was Hugo, "Sarah Tepper," she answered.

"Ms. Tepper, this is Tony Belvedere at New York Police Department forensics. Are you involved in any way with a Dr. Hugo Barnhill?"

"Who are you, again and how did you get this number?"

"I got the number from a diary found in Barnhill's office by detective Chekhov of the NYPD, who is investigating Barnhill's death. The last notation in Barnhill's diary just said NSA, the word 'Amerada' and this number."

Sarah was stunned. "Barnhill's death? When? How?" She slumped back in her chair.

"His computer blew up in his face last night and killed him. So tell me, are you involved in what he was working on?"

"What he was doing was classified and I shouldn't say any more. I don't know you."

"You can call NYPD and check me out. I have the remnants of Barnhill's computer and I'm trying to find out what happened and why. It's been ruled a homicide by NYPD so I got involved."

"Look," she looked at the name she had just written down, "Mr. Belvedere. This has been quite a shock to me. But if what you say is true and you have Barnhill's computer, you should turn it over to me immediately. I will need to deal with it."

"Problem is, Ms. Tepper, there were two other killings last week. One seems to be related to this one, so NYPD is not going to let the evidence or the case go easily."

"I know about those. We are pretty sure both of them are related, but I don't want to fight a turf war. I can't tell you anything about what Dr. Barnhill was working on because of its classification. In fact, I shouldn't have even confirmed that he was doing something for me. I have jurisdiction and can force you to send the computer to me. I'd rather not fight about it."

"Me neither. I'll talk to my boss and see what can be done. I'll get back to you this afternoon."

"Thanks, Mr. Belvedere. But before you hang up, did you find anything out?"

"Not really. The computer is too thin to house a bomb strong enough to do the damage that was done. I thought it may have been attached on the back but there doesn't appear to be any residue suggesting any explosive material we might expect. I do think the hard disk may be recoverable but with great difficulty. I asked about Barnhill because I wouldn't know what to be looking for if I succeed in dumping the data on the disk."

"That's why it's better if I do that. Get back to me as soon as you can, please," she pleaded.

"Will do. Talk to you later."

Shit, Sarah said to herself. What the fuck is going on? An NSA project called Amerada with no apparent owner, that no one knows anything about, a blocked account with no way in, three people killed with some relationship to the project, however small. What to do, she mumbled. She got up and started pacing very slowly. Hugo was only working for her two days. Was he killed because of his involvement. All of a sudden, Sarah realized that if people are so concerned about Amerada to kill, almost indiscriminately, she might be in danger herself. But how?

Maybe Conaghey's hit-and-run death was not an accident. Maybe the coincidence that his girlfriend was mugged and strangled a day later was relevant. Nothing was made of her death at the time. Just an unfortunate coincidence. But now, Sarah was beginning to sense real trouble.

Sarah answered Tony Belvedere's call back. "Where do we stand?" she asked.

"I can ship everything to your office by special courier. But I can't get it out until tomorrow. I need to finish the inventory and pack it up properly."

"Great. How did you get permission so easily?"

"Frankly, we're, that is, my boss, is a little worried that getting involved in something as strange as this might be very dangerous. And he's not one to take risks."

She laughed. "And NYPD let it go, just like that?"

"He didn't even ask them and he won't. He just decided that his excuse was that he didn't want to get involved in an NSA investigation because NSA has jurisdiction."

"I'll tell you, even though I shouldn't. I've got thoughts about my own involvement. Dr. Barnhill was only working on it a couple of days and was killed. Whoever in running this Amerada thing is very sensitive. And considering the situation, I don't know who to trust here."

"Let's keep in touch and keep our noses sniffing," he answered. "And be careful."

"I fully expect to. I'll keep you in the loop as much as I can, that is if you're interested. I really shouldn't because it's classified but I will, primarily for your safety."

"I appreciate that. But keep in mind that I am not a spy. I am well trained and might actually be of some help. Let me know when you get the shipment."

"OK," she laughed, "Talk to you soon." As soon as Sarah hung up, she called her boss. "Got a minute for me, Director?"

"What's up, Sarah?"

"I'd rather not discuss it on the phone."

"Fine, come on up."

Sarah closed the door to her office and as she walked out, Armand, her assistant, asked, "Going out?"

"Just going up to twelve to see Manson."

She got off the elevator and was signaled through the open door, closing it behind her before she sat down.

The director, Stuart Manson, watched Sarah close the door so carefully with a skeptical smile and then said, "What's up, Sarah? Something happen in congress to upset you?"

"No, sir." she replied in a voice that eliminated the smile from the director's face. "Something very strange is going on and I'm unsure what to do next."

"Sounds serious," he spoke with a patronizing tone. "Tell me."

"Two weeks ago, one of our agents, Paul Conaghey was found in the wooded area next to the West Side highway in New York, the result of a hit and run driver. What they found on his person was something about an NSA project called Amerada. I didn't pay much attention at the time. The New York police were working on it. Then the next day, his girlfriend was strangled after being mugged outside of their hotel."

The director perked up in his seat as if suddenly very interested. Sarah added, "Strange coincidence, wouldn't you say? I was still only marginally interested but felt interested enough to look into it. I tried to find out about this Amerada thing and discovered there was indeed an NSA account with that name. I tried to get into it but was denied access. No matter what I did, I couldn't get in. I asked around and no one knew who was responsible for the Amerada account."

"That's no problem, I can get you in. He picked up the telephone and dialed.

"No you can't," she stopped him. "Nobody can."

Manson spoke into the phone. "Can you get me into the Amerada account? We're working on something and we've been denied access." He waited a moment. "Never heard of it? Come on, Joe, don't break my balls." He waited again. "OK, I'll try." Looking at Sarah, "He never heard of it. You sure there is such a thing?"

Sarah remained poker-faced. "That's not all. It gets worse. I called an old techie who did work for us a few years ago, you probably remember, Hugo Barnhill."

"Yes I do remember him.. PhD right? Good guy, if I remember rightly. He was very good getting us into the Iranian websites."

"That's right. I called him day before yesterday and asked him to use his magic to get into this Amerada account."

"How'd he do?"

"New York PD called me this morning. He was killed last night in his office. His computer blew up in his face."

"What?" he sat up sharply. "What the fuck, sorry for the language."

"I've heard the word before." She continued, "So only a couple of days after getting a request to investigate Amerada, the investigator is killed."

"Do you have any ideas?"

"Well, I know already, I shouldn't trust anyone. You're the only one I've talked to about it. NYPD is sending the remnants of Barnhill's computer to me and from this point on, I will not discuss the Amerada affair any further. Don't ask me anything and I suggest that you don't discuss it further either. I will tell you when I get a handle on what's happening. Until I know something, I have no choice. I know it's not paranoid to consider my life at risk. I'm a happy desk jockey. If this Amerada thing is being watched so closely that even a hint of finding anything out gets one killed, well, that's fucking scary and I'm not used to it. So, I ask you please, this meeting never happened and you won't mention it again to anybody."

"Fair enough. What are you going to do?"

"Not a clue, yet. But I'll figure something out."

"Somehow though, you should keep me posted."

"I'll work something out." Sarah got up and left quickly to go back to her office. She stopped at the ladies room on the twelfth floor. She looked at her face with a certain vanity and was pleased that no wrinkles were evident. She still looked like the college girl of years earlier. She had recently realized that her job was dominating her life and she didn't like it.

She closed her office door after her and sat down. Things were popping into Sarah's head faster than she could process them.

How could Barnhill have been targeted so fast, even before he did anything? Killed before he had even done anything serious. Is someone listening to her conversations? Tapping her phone? Is there a mole in her department? She realized that she already had a virtual target on her back and had to be very careful. She got up and started pacing. She put on her coat and walked out.

"Going out?" Armand asked again.

"Shopping, Back in half hour." She went down to the Radio Shack in the building.

"I want two pre-paid Iphones and two cards with a hundred minutes each."

The clerk took two off the shelf with two sealed prepaid cards and started keying it into the computer. "The numbers are on the booklet that comes with each computer. Who should I make the bill out to?"

"Marilyn Monroe," she answered. "M O N R O E," she spelled it out.

He didn't bat an eye. "Email address?"

"Can't have it," she answered, nastily. When he was finished, he printed and handed her the bill and asked, "How will you pay, Ms. Monroe?"

Sarah looked at the bill. "I'll be right back. I want to get cash."

"We'll take a debit card, you know." he said.

"I know you will. I'll be right back." She went to the bank next door where she had an account and cashed a check for two thousand dollars. She came back into the Radio Shack where the clerk was waiting on someone else. She waited patiently and when he was ready for her, she peeled off several hundred dollar bills and handed them to him.

He gave her the change and a shopping bag with her telephones. "Have a nice day Ms. Monroe and thanks for shopping with us;"

"Do you have a bag that doesn't say Radio Shack?" He looked at her funny. "Please?"

He reached under the counter and pulled out a brown paper bag. "Will this work for you, Ms. Monroe?"

"Perfect," She transferred the phones. "Thanks."

You're quite welcome," he said, automatically, a result of his training.

Sarah went back up to her office without talking to anyone, not even Armand who looked at her, but said nothing. She picked up her desk phone and called security. "Melvin, I need someone to do a scan of my office. When can you do it? Great, I'll wait for him." While she was waiting, she unpacked both phones and inserted the prepaid chips into each of the phones and plugged them in to be charged. As soon as she finished, she answered the knock on her office door and let the security technician in.

"I'm Charlie. Melvin sent me. You suspect anything in particular, Ms. Tepper?"

"Nah, call me Sarah," she interjected, then said, "Just a routine check. I decide to do it when I think of it. I keep putting it off so I made up my mind it was time."

She sat and watched while Charlie ran his sensors over everything. After about forty-five minutes, he looked up and said, "You're clean."

"Phone, too?"

"Yup. Nothing in the phone either. But if you are worried about something in particular, I would turn off my computer if I were you, anytime I didn't want to be detected. In fact, I would put a piece of tape over the camera unless you're a Skype fanatic. You never know who might be watching."

"They can do that?"

"You have no idea what can be done."

"Thanks, Charlie, and regards to Melvin."

"Will do," He snapped the clasps on his tool box and waved himself out the door.

Sarah got up and closed the door. So if my phone isn't tapped and there's no listening devices, how did whoever it was, find out about Barnhill, she thought. Was it my computer? Was it because he tried to access the Amerada account? Something is very rotten in DC. From here on, nothing of any consequence on my regular phone or cell. She took a piece of adhesive tape from her desk drawer and covered the camera on top of her Imac. She opened the door and called Armand. "Come in," she waved.

He got up and went in. "What's up, Sarah?"

"Not much. I need round trip ticket to New York, tonight and a hotel."

"Plane or train?"

"I prefer train. Tonight whatever's available and tomorrow return sometime in the afternoon."

"Reason for the trip?"

"Shopping. I need a break. But put down visit to NYPD so no one asks."

He smiled, "You got it Boss. I'll arrange it."

"Thanks. Close the door after you." She took one of her pre-paid phones and called Tony Belvedere. "Mr. Belvedere, Sarah Tepper. I'm coming up to NewYork tonight. Can I see you in the morning, about nine?"

"Sure, Ms. Tepper. Reason?"

"I'll tell you when I see you. Pick a place to meet. I don't want to come to your office."

"OK, where are you staying tonight?" he asked.

"The Lucerne on West 79ᵗʰ Street."

Tony thought for a few seconds, "How about Starbucks on 79ᵗʰ Street?"

""Great, see you at nine. That OK?"

"How will I know you?"

"I'll wear a yellow scarf. And you?"

"I'm the good-looking guy with premature steel gray hair."

She laughed, "Got it. I hope we agree on the good-looking part so I'll recognize you. Otherwise you'll have to find me. See you tomorrow." She plugged the phone back into the charger. New York City, Next Morning

Next morning

Tony was drumming his fingers on the table while sipping his coffee. He had been at Starbucks since twenty to nine. Many things had gone through his head since yesterday and he vacillated from curiosity to a hint of fear. When he saw Sarah with the yellow scarf come in the door, he got up to meet her and led her to the table he was sitting at."Tony Belvedere, What are you drinking?" he asked.

She put out her hand. "Sarah Tepper, call me Sarah, please. Coffee with milk and a cinnamon pastry," she said as she took her coat off. "You are good-looking. We agree on that. Be right back," she added.

He smiled and took her hand. "Tony, please," he said, "Sit, I'll get your bun." He brought the coffee and put the bun on the table. When she came back he commented, "Voila. You're better looking than I thought you would be."

"What did you expect? Tell me."

"Well, you know. NSA. Career bureaucrat. A regular plain Jane. Dowdy. A little on the chubby side."

"Enough, enough. Unfortunately, I am married to my job, but I do look in the mirror and can't stand 'plain' and try not to be. Changing the subject, let me tell you why I'm here."

He interjected, "I've got to say, I'm curious and at the same time worried. Three people have died that have had even the slightest connection to this Amerada thing, whatever it is."

"I have to agree so you do know why. The thing that's so scary is that Dr. Barnhill was barely involved. I just told him what I was looking for, two days ago. I'm sure he was barely up to speed before he was killed. I made a ten minute innocuous phone call describing my problem, which seemed, at the time, a simple one. I was blocked from getting into one of our accounts. The following night, not even night, evening according to your call, his computer blew up and killed him. He hadn't even started anything yet."

"Someone tapping your phone?"

"Had it checked and had my office scanned. Nothing." She shook her head. "Nada."

"Anybody nosing around?"

"I don't know and wasn't aware of anyone. That's why I decided to see you in person – and at Starbucks. I have no fucking clue what's going on and frankly, I don't know who I can trust. Until I can get my arms around this, I'm going to be a wreck."

"You're not new in your job. Why should this bother you so intensely?"

"I've been with NSA for twelve years but I've always had an administrative job. I was never in a risky situation. I was never trained for it. This has got me scared because I don't know anything, absolutely nothing, and three people have been killed. Barnhill was killed and I'm sure he hadn't found anything out yet."

"You don't know that. Maybe he did discover something."

"No, I don't think so. He would have called me right away."

"Let me suggest something. I have a friend, an Italian. I met him at a conference at MIT several years ago and we've become very good friends. He's somewhat of a forensic genius, especially with technology."

"I can't do that."

"Wait, hear me out. He works for the Italian government but the bureaucratic bullshit bores him so like a regular Sherlock Holmes that needs stimulation, he takes on whatever puzzles present themselves."

Sarah answered after a long pregnant pause. "I don't know."

"Let's do it this way," Tony said. "I can call him and tell him what happened with Barnhill's computer and your lockout at Amerada and tell him to do his thing. He's in Italy and who would know?"

Sarah handed one of her new prepaid phones to Tony. "Call him now, on this phone. I'll listen in but don't put it on speaker."

Tony looked at her, then took out his phone to get the number, and called. Alberto DeSanctis answered, *"Pronto, sono DeSanctis."*

"Alberto, sono Tony Belvedere da New York. Come stai?"

"*Favoloso, amico mio. E tu?*"

"*Senti, parliamo in Inglese. Ho qui un amica chi vuol capire.*"

"*Va bene.* Talk to me,"

"I'm great. Tell me, are you still looking for challenges to relieve your bureaucratic boredom? If so, I've got one for you."

"Of course. *Comé no?* Why not? Tell me."

Tony looked at Sarah. "You want to tell him, or shall I?"

"You do it. If I think I should jump in, I will."

Tony explained the situation in as much detail as he knew. Finally Alberto answered."What should I do when I discover anything or want to ask questions?"

"Call back at this number and ask for the lady with the yellow scarf." He smiled at Sarah.

"Sounds like a movie. Is there a password?"

"No, just a little precaution. We're worried, as you can imagine."

"Who will I be talking to?"

"Her name is Sarah and she's at a US government office."

"*Bene.* I won't ask any more. Tell her I'll call as soon as I learn anything. Tell me, Tony. Is there any chance you can send me the hard drive and a photo of the blown up computer? That really interests me."

Tony looked at Sarah. "He would like the hard drive from the Barnhill computer. Can I send it to him?"

Sarah thought for a moment. "Better for it to be out of the country, don't you think? Send it with no return address."

"OK Alberto. Where should I send it?"

"Send it to my home in a plain brown wrapper. You know the address."

"Yes. Maybe we can use this as an excuse to get together. It's been a while."

"Yes it has. You know I'm going to be a father. You have to meet my wife."

"Wow, how did that happen? Last we spoke was only about six months ago."

"I'll tell you all when I see you. Meanwhile, send it to me. Ciao."

"*Ciao, Alberto, ci sentiamo.*" Turning to Sarah. "Here's your phone. I'll send the hard drive to him and the computer itself to you. Is that OK?"

"Almost sounds like we're making some progress, even if we aren't. How come you're so fluent in Italian?"

"Italian's my first language. You don't hear any accent?

"Maybe now that you've told me."

"Came here when I was a teenager. What time are you leaving later?"

"I planned to take the 7:30 out of Penn Station."

"Great. Let's have an early dinner about 5:30."

"You mean like a date?"

He chuckled, "Yeah, a date. Meet me at Keen's Steakhouse, on 36th Street, near 7th avenue, spitting distance from Penn Station."

"I behave myself on the first date. Is that OK?"

"Has to be. Unless you stay over or want me to come down to Washington with you tonight."

"Just dinner," she quipped. "If you feel deprived, we can split the tab."

"No. It'll be worth it anyway. It's on me," he said. She smiled, looked at him coquettishly and got up to leave.

"See you at 5:30."

Tony sat there and watched her leave. There was something about her. It wasn't her looks, although she was pretty. No, it was as George Harrison wrote, something about the way she walked. He finished his coffee and went to his office. Without waiting, he took his tool kit out and put the computer remnants on the table. Before doing anything, he took several photographs of the wrecked computer and remains including some closeups. He worked with great difficult but eventually got the hard drive out. The top was damaged badly, melted. Looking at the back he thought, maybe Alberto can get something out of this. I know I wouldn't be able to. He gingerly put it in a plastic bag and wrapped it in bubble wrap fixing it with packing tape. He looked around the office for a small box and found a small Amazon box in his closet. It was perfect. He packed the drive in the box and got a label from his desk and addressed it. He wrote on the box, *campione, senza valore* – sample, no value - to get it past customs in Italy without being opened. But more important, it would avoid any special attention. He took the box and went right down to the post office. He didn't trust his mailroom.

Tony called Randy Chekhov. "Hey Randy, Tony at forensics. How you doing on the Barnhill matter?"

"Nothing so far. No sign of anyone in his office. You already know the only prints found were his. The other two deaths are a lost cause. Anything on the computer?"

"Nah. Looks like a total loss," he lied. "I keep working on it. Too early to give up, yet. I'll let you know if I find something. You do the same, OK?"

"Will do. Take care."

Tony was early at Keen's and Sarah was punctual as usual. He was waiting for her at the bar. "What are you drinking?" she asked, looking at his stemmed glass.

"Just nursing a red wine. What would you like?"

"I'll have the same. Don't drink much, only wine and mostly with meals."

"Me neither. But I couldn't sit at the bar waiting for you with a glass of water. Besides, I'm Italian. I need wine to function."

She smiled. He waved at the bartender who came over and just looked at him. "Another cabernet for my lady, please." Without a word, he brought one over and set it in front of Sarah. "We have reservations so let's sit at the table. Take the wine with you." At the table, Tony commented, "No business at dinner, right?"

"Agreed. But you have to tell me about yourself." She got right to the point.

"I feel like I'm in an opera. You ever see La Boheme?"

"No, I'm a classical music lover but opera doesn't do it for me."

"Mimi, who lives upstairs, comes to Rodolfo's apartment, needing a light because her candle went out. She drops her key and with both of them looking for it, he touches her cold hand which obviously leads him to tell her his life story."

"Really, that's all it takes?"

"It's opera," he emphasized. "Then he asks her to tell him about herself which she does. They then sing a love duet and march off to the cafe together, already hopelessly in love."

"Well, I don't expect your life story but a little about you would be interesting. How old are you, for example?"

"Thirty eight. Born in Sondrio, northern Italy. Came here as a teenager with my parents and younger sister, Daniela.. Always lived in New York. I went to Columbia, degree in physics. Graduate school at Princeton, two years, got MA. Never finished PhD. I was fed up with school."

"No wife, girl friend?"

"Nope. Had a serious relationship but it broke up five years ago Now you."

"Thirty-six. Born and raised in Jacksonville, Florida. Scholarship to Yale, BS in psychology. Got MA in history at Florida State. Went to work for NSA as an analyst. Been there ever since. Never married, one serious relationship many years ago, broke my heart."

"How come? An attractive woman like you."

"How come what?"

"How come no permanent mate, boy friend, lover?"

Sarah shrugged. "Involved in my work too much."

"Yeah, but you got hormones like everyone else."

She laughed, "This kind of work can mitigate them beyond recognition."

"Too bad. Some guy is missing out, unless you're gay."

"No, no fucking way. Just attenuated hormones."

"I know I said no business talk but one question. Do you have any idea what you're going to do?"

"No. I've got four hours on a train and the whole night to think about it. Meanwhile, take this phone." She pulled one of the pre-paids out of her purse. "And use it for anything about our problem. I have the other one." She took the other phone out and dialed the one she gave Tony. "Now you have my number. I just hope this works and keeps us isolated."

"It should."

The dinner was very enjoyable. Apparently both of them were hungry for companionship. When they finished dessert, Tony looked at his watch. "We have plenty of time. I'll walk you over to Penn Station."

"Thanks, I appreciate that. I hate trying to figure out where the train is by myself."

"That's not my expertise and it's not my purpose but I'll try to help. I am thoroughly enjoying the evening and it's been a while." He took her arm and they walked slowly to Penn Station making small talk. "Next time you come, I'll take you to the opera, assuming of course a suitable one is showing for a novice."

"I've never been. But I've heard some awful singing that's turned me off."

"Bad singing will do that. I'll check the voices before I drag you to the Met." He looked up at the board and pointed. "There's your train 7:30 to Washington, track 21. It's that way."

"Thanks for dinner." she said, "and the company. It took some of the tension of this problem off. But now I have hours to think about it."

"Don't worry, we'll figure it out."

"We?"

"Of course. I'm involved whether you like it or not."

"Yeah, OK, but we have to figure it out without getting killed," she added. "I should make you apply for security clearance to keep you involved but I'm going to skip it because I don't want anyone in my office to know about your involvement.

I can get my hands slapped for that but it's better than getting killed."

"Just be careful and pretend to be totally uninterested while we look into things. Alberto will be a big help. I guarantee it. He kind of anticipates needs."

"I hope so. I'll take your word for it" She got on the train and sat next to the window where she saw him wave and leave the station."

The ride back to Washington seemed an eternity for Sarah. She knew herself. Forcing a plan of action never worked for her. She just let her unconscious mind work without disturbing it and a plan would evolve and make its way to her consciousness. When she did that, things usually worked out. If she forced it, what came out was usually worth only to show she was working. In this situation, that wasn't the case. This wasn't a reality show. She needed a real plan that worked, so she just let her mental synapses cook by themselves.

CHAPTER II

Theodore

The well-dressed stocky man walked around to the back of the old building, took off his hat exposing his shiny bald head and knocked on the door. A tall scarecrow-like man answered the door and without a word, let the man in.

"Good evening, Teddy," he said. "I came to see how you're doing."

"I told you my name is Theodore, Mr. Flint. I don't like to be called Teddy."

Flint put his hat on the coffee table and sat down on the ragged couch. "Yes, Theodore. Tell me what's going on. There is a lot at stake and I can't afford any screwups"

"As best I can tell, there's been very little activity regarding the account. No one has tried to access it since Barnhill was, uh, eliminated. I am watching very carefully. It would seem as if they have lost interest."

"That doesn't seem possible. Especially since they are aware that the three deaths involve Amerada. Tell me Theodore, do you always know if someone is trying to access the account?"

"Not always. I can tell if someone is trying and denied access but I don't know for sure who is trying. Unless I happen to be watching at the time I can go after the source. I certainly know if someone succeeds in getting in but they have to stay on the account while I'm watching, for me to trace who it is. But I've been able to get into any computer we think might be trouble and watch what they are doing and saying. I can also get information from their cell phones. So I can monitor what's going on. And since Barnhill, nothing. I can get to the computers of this Tepper woman and her boss. I have not been able to get into the right

NYPD computer. If necessary, I have their email addresses and can do the same thing as I did to Barnhill, if another killing would help things."

"I don't think so. In fact it would make things worse. We are counting on your expertise Theodore. We have two weeks left. You will let me know if we have anything to worry about, won't you? You, too, have a large vested interest in the success."

"I know, I know. I'm on it. Don't worry."

"Fine." He got up and put on his hat. "You know how to reach me. If there is any doubt, you call me." He said it as a question.

"Yes, I know." He opened the door for the stocky man and closed it after him. Theodore did not trust Flint. Anyone who could order a kill without compunction was not to be trusted. He had to figure a way to protect himself in case he was threatened with a double-cross.Theodore told himself there was nothing to stop him from killing me when the deal is concluded instead of paying. I have to create some insurance and let him know so he doesn't screw me. He paced back and forth and after a few minutes, sat at his computer. He could see that no one had yet been able to get into the account. He also knew that it was just a matter of time with their resources that someone would break into the site. He had to watch for that. He had to be attentive for only two weeks more. After that, vacation.

One Day Later

Sarah got an idea. She had sent emails to the department heads asking about Amerada. No one answered. Was it really possible that not one of them knew anything about it? She didn't want to get anyone bent out of shape by sending another request, indicating this was still under investigation. But what if she did it backwards? She could send an email out to the department heads saying the Amerada account was a non-problem and thanks for their help. If anyone was involved they would have to try to find out what we had discovered, if anything. She could say it was nothing, a false alarm, to throw the scent off but the culprit might just give himself away. In fact just by asking might be an indication of involvement.

She crafted the email carefully for all department heads.

Subject. Amerada website.

Just to advise. The Amerada website I inquired about the other day turned out to be nothing. In these terrorist days, we can't leave any stone unturned so we sometimes overreact. Thanks for your help and sorry to have bothered you.

Sarah Tepper

She read it over three times to be sure then sent it out from her computer. She copied her boss and to her surprise, he called her immediately.

"The Amerada thing is nothing?"

She thought for a minute because she was not sure how she should answer him. It's not that she didn't trust him, she just thought that he has no sense of confidentiality. She always felt he didn't know when to shut up. "Just a dummy site. Nothing. I'm dropping the matter."

"Great, nice work keeping after it."

"Thanks, Director." She felt guilty receiving the compliment. She called Tony from her prepaid phone and told him what she had done.

"Sounds like a very clever idea to me. What will you do if someone gets curious?"

"Tell him what I told my boss. That it's a dummy website with nothing on it. Then I'll see what kind or reaction I get from that."

"You think you'll be believed?"

"Oh yeah, I'm an expert at playing dumb."

"From a Yalette, or whatever they're called."

"Lots of dumb Yale graduates. I wouldn't be so unusual. And don't ask me to name any."

He laughed. "You're right. I could name a few myself. Let me know if anyone bites."

"I sure will. I might even come back to New York to tell you. The phone is not to be trusted, right?"

"Even better. But for the moment, I'll accept a phone call."

"Anything from your friend, yet?"

"I'll come down and tell you as soon as I hear."

"Funny, funny. Keep in touch. Talk to you soon."

Sarah's prepaid phone rang when she hung up, which surprised her. "Hello," she said gingerly.

"Sarah, this is your friend Alberto."

"Alberto, good to hear from you. I didn't expect it so soon. Do you have questions?"

"No. I have information for you."

"I'm listening."

"I have succeeded in getting into the uh, account. It was not so difficult. I will give you the password. Are you ready to write?"

"Ready."

"D o l l a r then three dollar signs. You got it?"

"Yes. How did you manage it so fast?"

"Ah. I have my ways. But listen, Sarah. There is nothing in the account but a single file which is passworded and encrypted. I have downloaded it to see if I can open it."

"You have to be careful Alberto. If whoever is monitoring access finds out where it's coming from..."

"Not to worry. If they find out, they will be frustrated. The computer will be totally undetectable. But if you are concerned, do not access the account. There is no need anyway. The file name on the site is *MoneySource.pdf.* I have already downloaded it and there's no need for me to enter the account again. Unless you can decrypt the file, there is no need for you to risk access either."

"We could certainly decrypt it but I don't know whom to trust."

"It will not be easy for anyone to decrypt, even at your organization. If you are stuck for trusting someone, let me try. If you wish, I can email the file to you which will avoid the necessity for you to access the account. Do you want me to? By the way, I have not received the hard drive yet from Tony."

"He only sent it yesterday so I don't expect you to get it for several days yet. As far as the file goes, don't send me a copy. I would rather not have it here."

"OK. I will keep in touch. May I continue to use this phone?"

"Yes, it's a prepaid unlisted phone."

"Ah good. I will be in touch. I must hang up now. *Ciao.*"

Sarah was ecstatic. She was making progress and she could still be passive without any attempt to access. But would Alberto's access alert whoever it is that's watching? That might be a good thing. Sometime when you rustle the bushes, the birds fly out.

The day was passing quickly and uneventfully. Sarah was more relaxed knowing that things were moving along but she didn't have to do anything. When Armand knocked on her door, she looked at the clock realizing that her day was almost over. "What's up, Armand?"

"A Henry Stafford is here and wants to see you. He's a division head."

"Show him in." Stafford was a sixtyish man, a little sloppy in his dress with balding head and tousled hair. "Nice to meet you Henry." She stood up. "After all this time, you would think our paths would have crossed by now. Sit, please. What can I do for you?"

"Nice to meet you, too, Sarah. I got your email this morning about the Amerada thing. What was that all about?"

"Nothing really. When I came upon it, it was a puzzle because I never saw it before"

"What was it? I see that you let it go."

"It turned out to be a dummy account with nothing. As I said in my email, these terrorist times some of us tend to overreact."

"How did you happen to find it?"

"I don't remember exactly. It was by accident, cleaning up some old stuff to be archived. When I found it, I just routinely looked to see what was in it and was denied access. As you can imagine, that raised a flag."

He faked a laugh. "I can understand that. But you're sure it's nothing?"

"Sure. Why do you ask?"

"As you said, some of us overreact. I'm one of them. But if you're sure it's nothing, 'nuff said." He got up to leave. "Nice to meet you. And if anything else turns up, consider me a companion over-reactor."

"Take care, Henry," she said as he walked out.

"Door closed?" he asked.

"Yes, thanks." Sarah thought to herself. Was this a break or just a coincidence? None of the other division heads gave a shit. Why would he, especially when she said it was nothing in her email? She turned to her computer and went to access his personnel record. Who was this Henry Stafford? When she found it, she realized it was very large so she downloaded it onto a thumb drive to take home. Studying would take time. She put the drive in her purse and got up.

Coat on, she told Armand, "Got some errands to run. See you in the morning."

"G'nite, Sarah," he replied

The Next Day

The stocky man answered his phone, "Hello."

"Herman, Stafford here."

"Ah, yes, Henry. What can I do for you."

"As you suggested, Herman, I checked out the Tepper woman. She seems to have lost interest in Amerada, but I'm not sure yet."

"Theodore told me that he did not detect any aggressive investigating on her part. It seemed strange to me since she knows that there were three deaths related somehow to a thing called Amerada, especially the Barnhill death."

"Perhaps she's not as diligent an employee as we worried about. We have to be careful not to overreact because of guilt. We all have to assume our non-involvement and believe it enough to put on a good act. We only have two weeks and then we're finished."

"You know, Mr. Stafford, Barnhill's death was really scary. Maybe she's just afraid."

"That's possible but that's not the impression I got from her. Unless I see otherwise or you pick up on something from your end, I think she's not a problem."

"OK Mr. Stafford. I'll trust your judgement for the moment. Thanks for letting me know."

The next morning, Henry Stafford paid a visit to Stuart Manson. He was hoping to ensure that his evaluation of Sarah was realistic. He was a thorough man and didn't like to leave things hanging. "Stuart, how've you been?"

"Great, Henry. It's been a while. What brings you here?"

"I went to see your Sarah Tepper. Quite a woman."

"Oh. Why your interest in Sarah? You're not really age appropriate," he laughed.

"No, nothing like that. I got her email about this Amerada thing and I was curious. She said it was nothing. What do you think?"

"She does her job She told me she's dropping it because it seems to be nothing. I can't see any reason not to believe her. She's pretty thorough. You think otherwise?"

"No, just a worrywart. Don't want anything serious to fall through the cracks."

"I'm sure it's nothing. She's good at her job."

"Thanks. I'd be interested if it turns out different. Keep me in the loop."

"Sure. No problem."

"Take care, Stuart."

When he was sure Stafford was gone, he called Sarah. "Sarah, Henry Stafford just left me. He asked whether I agreed with your finding on the Amerada thing. Why would he do that? What's his interest?"

Sarah was surprised, not that Stafford was curious about Amerada, but that he double checked to be sure of Sarah. "I don't know, Director. He said he was one of those over-reactors, like me. I told him it was nothing."

"He didn't seem to believe you. Or at least wanted verification."

"That's either strange or annoying, or both," she answered. "I've got enough on my plate. I can't follow non-leads."

"I told him you're thorough and that I trust your conclusion."

"Next time you see him, you can tell him for me that I'm pissed that he felt he had to check up on me."

"Come on, Sarah. Don't get yourself in a snit. I'm sure he didn't mean anything by it."

"OK, I'll drop it. Thanks for telling me though." Sarah had spent hours going through Henry Stafford's file the night before. The only thing she found of any consequence, and it was significant, was that Henry Stafford was broke and had a negative net worth. He was paying his ex-wife alimony but he had been, at one time, a very wealthy man. She tried without success to find out how he wound up in such dire straits. But that he was financially challenged was obvious. Was Amerada some scheme to make money, she wondered? And if so, how and how much? And who else was involved? It must be a huge amount of money if they are so sensitive that they kill anyone involved. Now she was getting anxious and was hoping that Alberto succeeded in decrypting the *MoneySource.pdf* file.

CHAPTER III

Theodore's apartment

Theodore perked up when he saw a breach in the Amerada account. Someone had gotten in, but how? He got to work and found that the breach came from Italy. He was surprised. But when he used his usual method to find out who and where, he was blocked. No matter how hard he tried, he couldn't break through. He called Herman Flint, who answered immediately.

"Mr. Flint, this is Theodore. There's been a breach of Amerada. Someone got into the account."

"Who was it? Not the Tepper woman?"

"No. I can't find out anything except that the computer that got in was in Italy.

"Italy? That's weird and disturbing."

"When I try to locate it the usual way, I can't. I have to find another method."

"We are paying you to know, Theodore. So you better find out who." Herman hung up and called Henry Stafford and without mentioning his name, he said,. "Theodore has detected a breach in Amerada coming from Italy but can't find out who or where yet. I thought you should know."

"We must find out. Our complete secrecy must be preserved or we will fail. I'm not worried yet because the file is encrypted."

"But someone with the talent and tools to break into Amerada might also be able to decrypt the file."

"That, my dear man, would be a disaster. It would require more talent than the break-in. The encryption is 64 bit, very secure. Nevertheless, give Theodore a kick. We must find out."

"I'll try. That's all I can do."

The Next Day

Sarah answered her anonymous phone. "Hello?"

"Sarah. This is Alberto. Someone picked up on my entry into Amerada and tried to find out who. The only thing they found out was that the breach came from Italy. That must have confused them. They didn't have any success finding me but I was able to ascertain that the location of the computer trying to check on me was in Arlington, Virginia. I will try to find out more. But I called to warn you again not to try to get into the account. Whoever is involved is monitoring it carefully. I have downloaded the encrypted file so that I no longer need to enter the account. My lack of interest may calm them."

"Thanks Alberto. Any luck with the file?"

"No, that's difficult. I'm sure it will take me a while."

"Tell me Alberto. Can you think of a reason that a rogue group involved in something illicit or illegal would create an NSA website and risk discovery?

"That's easy, Sarah. First, hidden in plain view is a possibility. Secondly, if the culprits work at NSA, they can control it better. Third and probably most important, a restricted NSA account is much harder to break into than any other. We've found that out."

Sarah thought it made sense. "Thanks again, Alberto, and keep in touch." Sarah put the secure telephone in her purse. She did not want to leave it around. She had no idea who was watching or listening or how. The situation was very stressful.

Theodore's Apartment

Herman knocked on Theodore's apartment door. He answered immediately. Without saying anything, Herman walked in, removed his hat and sat down. "Theodore. We are concerned about the breach, very concerned. Have you found out, yet, who got into the website?"

Theodore was obviously nervous. "I have not been able to break through yet. But don't worry, when I do, if we consider it still a problem, I can take care of things like I did with Barnhill."

"I know you can do that. But if you can't find out who's doing it and obtain the email address, your lethal tool is useless."

"I'll find out. Don't worry."

"I always worry when someone tells me not to worry," he said very quietly and then added. "Like I never believe someone who tells me "believe me." Mr. Stafford is not a patient man and not knowing who is doing this is a risk we don't want to take. Must we get someone else? You know that if Mr. Stafford recommends we find another expert, Galahad doesn't like to leave loose ends and he doesn't like to pay two people."

"I'll find out very soon."

Herman got up, put on his hat and said, "Yes, it must be very soon. A word to the wise Theodore," he added as he left.

A telephone call

The man with the very thick Russian accent but perfect English grammar recognized the voice on the other end. "What can I do for you Mr. ..."

He was interrupted, "Please, no names. I want to know where we stand with our proposal. There are others interested and we want to conclude the deal as quickly as possible."

"I told you that I needed two weeks and that is still valid."

"I understand. I just want to emphasize that there is no extension. We have two other customers. They are not willing to pay quite as much as you are but we are more interested in closing a deal quickly and are willing to sacrifice something, if necessary, for an expeditious conclusion. The longer we wait, the greater the risk of discovery and that would be bad for both of us."

"I know that, and nothing has changed. The amount and the time frame are as I have said. There are eleven days left and I am sure we will conclude things by then."

The voice added, "There have been several attempts to find out what we are doing and we have had to take drastic measures to protect ourselves. So we are at great risk. If we are discovered, evidently there will be no deal. It would help both of us considerably if you could conclude even earlier."

"That is possible but I do not want to promise something I cannot guarantee."

"A guarantee is not necessary. But we would appreciate trying to get things approved earlier."

"You shall hear from me, soon"

"Thank you" He hung up and called Stafford. "Henry, I just spoke to our customer and explained our sense of urgency to expedite the deal sooner and that there is no possibility of extension. He agreed to try and assured me that at worst, he will meet his promised date."

"That's good," Henry said. "I am not calm about our situation. Do you trust him?"

"I have no reason to assume anything else. He obviously wants what we have very anxiously."

"Is the Tepper woman still doing nothing?"

"Nothing that I have heard, and I try to pay attention. She seems to really believe it's a non-item. Have you seen anything?"

"No, but somehow even with my attempts to verify it, I find it hard to accept that she's ignoring it. She's no dope. But so far, I have seen nothing to indicate any interest."

"OK, then, keep in touch, please."

Sarah's Office

"Sarah, this is Stuart."

"Hi. What's up?"

"I've been trying to get into this Amerada account with no luck. How did you manage it?"

Sarah was taken aback. and answered the only way she could. "I didn't actually do it myself. I had a techie hack into it and saw that there was nothing there. While it would be nice to know whose it is, since nothing is in it, I haven't got the time to chase after it for curiosity's sake. Why are you trying to get into it anyway?"

"Truth is Stafford's visit yesterday bugged me a little. First of all, it's none of his business if it's not his account. Second, why is he trying to verify what you're doing?"

"Probably just nosy. For the same reason you are trying to verify. Everyone around here is paranoid. No one believes anybody. From you, I accept that. You're my boss. But Stafford, no way. But working at NSA does that, don't you think?" Sarah had difficulty getting these words out. Stafford's interest was in her mind not paranoid but self-serving. He was more involved is something illicit, she sensed.

"Maybe you're right but it still bugs me nevertheless."

"If you really want to get into it, I could get the password from my techie."

"I'll let you know. For the moment, I haven't got the time either. Talk to you later." He hung up brusquely

That was a little weird, but Sarah breathed a sigh of relief. If I gave him the password, he would find the file. That wouldn't work. I would have to delete the file in the account. I wonder, she thought. What would happen if Alberto deleted the file from the account?. He has a copy of it. That might just create a small panic, enough to make them reveal themselves. She got up and started pacing."

Armand could see her pacing through the opaque glass of the door and opened it. He stuck his head in. "You OK, Sarah?" he said.

"I'm fine. Just thinking over a few things. Why?"

"I could see you pacing through the glass. Is there something I can do?"

She smiled. "Just nervous energy."

"You're not still worried about the Barnhill death, are you?"

That was a funny question from Armand, she thought. He never cared about me before. He always kept to himself and did what was asked. "Not really. I put that to bed as just a homicide and I'm letting the New York police deal with it. I doubt it had anything to do with what's going on here."

"If you need anything, I'm here."

That too was out of character. She thought, Armand is efficient but not a gracious sort. He's not someone I would have a beer with. That's why I like him. "I know, thanks for asking." Very strange, she thought. Maybe I'm worrying him to where he is suddenly concerned. Was I giving off needy vibes? Or am I just being paranoid like everyone else here because of what I'm hiding about Amerada?

She called Tony, "Hey, what's up Sarah? Miss me?"

"Could be. Seriously, Tony, I had a thought. What would you think about having Alberto delete the file from the Amerada account? It could shake things up, don't you think?

Tony thought for a minute. "It might shake things up too much. What gave you the idea to do that?"

"My boss came to see me and asked about the account. He was freaked out about Stafford's interest and tried to get into the account without success. I could let him in – Alberto gave me the password – but he'll see the file and that would open a can of worms. If he asks me again, I would like to be able to let him in."

"You know, there might be a better way. Alberto could delete the file and substitute an innocuous one that isn't passworded or encrypted. Then the Amerada bad guys wouldn't notice anything unless they had reason to believe there was tampering or they're extra cautious. In fact, to be safer, if Alberto finds out the file password, he could put it on a new file and encrypt the file. It's not likely they would decrypt the file to check it."

"True," she said.

"Listen, Sarah, I wouldn't admit you had the password. Try to keep him out of the file. What's to say he wouldn't be at risk for poking into the account?"

"Yeah maybe, but they wouldn't have it so easy. This place is like a fortress."

"You mean like the French Maginot line the the Germans marched around. Until we find out how the Barnhill murder was committed, I'm not comfortable with the fortress defense. By the way, Alberto called me. He got the hard drive and my photos already."

"Great. Hopefully, he'll find something useful."

"Let me think about the file. Don't do anything yet," Tony said.

"All right. I can wait. Any news on the Barnhill front?"

"Nothing. Absolutely nothing, for that matter, to identify someone other than Barnhill in his office or on his computer. That's what is so strange. How the fuck did someone bomb him? We don't know how careless he might have been about leaving his office open. And unfortunately, we can't ask him. They are frustrated primarily because they are under pressure. Whenever there is a hint of a serial killing and the press gets on their ass, they don't like to tell reporters they have no clue."

"That's the only thing that gives me pause here. They ask how come I'm not interested in Amerada when there have been three killings but even if the other two are coincidental, the Barnhill case is hard to dodge."

"How do you manage that?" he asked her.

"I just behave like an incompetent employee with no real curiosity. I make the stupid assumption that Barnhill's death was caused by, perhaps, one of his other clients."

"Doesn't bother your feminine ego?"

"I don't have to prove my intellectual capacity. When we get it figured out, I'll take a huge bow and show how clever I am."

Tony laughed. "You are one interesting lady."

"You have no idea," she replied. "No idea."

"Gotta go now. I'll call you later when I've had time to mull your idea over."

"Love to hear from you," she said sexily and hung up the phone. She was careful to put the phone back in her purse.

Stafford's Apartment

Stafford answered his phone. "I'm getting nervous. I just find it hard to believe that Tepper is so incompetent. She must be hiding her involvement."

The voice answered quietly, "I cannot talk right now, too dangerous. But I have seen or heard nothing that would indicate any activity. Besides, don't you think Theodore would catch it?"

"I don't trust him. I'm sure if they find him out, he will throw all of us under the bus," Stafford said.

"I agree, but I'm confident he will do his job and they won't find him. He has too much at stake. Keep your calm and all will go well."

"I hear you, but I'm still not comfortable," Stafford replied.

"What would make you comfortable?"

"I don't know. I just wish the transaction was over."

Stafford hung up and sat back in his chair and went over things in his head. Can I can call Manson again and see if anything is happening?. He would begin to wonder why I'm so interested. I am going to access the account and make sure everything is OK. There's nothing much to see, I know but I'm afraid I would be putting myself at risk with Theodore monitoring access. He doesn't think because Flint doesn't want him to. To Theodore, if it moves, shoot it and ask questions later. He picked up his telephone.

"Herman, this is Stafford. I am going into the account. Would you please inform Theodore so he's aware of it."

"I shall. Why are you going into the account?"

"Just a routine check to make sure the merchandise is there."

"OK. Give me twenty minutes. If you don't hear from me, things are good."

"Thanks Herman, bye." Stafford looked at his watch and walked over to the window. After a few minutes, he sat down at his computer and accessed the New York Times online. After going through it, he checked his watch again and logged into Amerada. He saw that the file was still there and tried to access it. The reply was to enter password. He frowned. Things are in order, he thought, but thought to himself he would really like to have the password to the file. Now if that Russian would only move his ass, I could be out of here.

Manson's office

Stuart Manson was an insecure man. Stafford's concern about Amerada made him feel like he wasn't doing his job. He never paid much attention to things anyway. Sarah had been with him so long and he gives her a long leash. But every once in a while, his conscience makes him wonder if he's really necessary. "Sarah, I've been thinking about this Amerada account. Can you get me the password, I want to get into it."

Sarah was taken aback. "Why the interest, Boss? Don't you trust me either?"

"Of course, I trust you. I just think I should be more involved. After all, people have been killed."

"We gave Barnhill an assignment, sure, but he had a lot of clients. We can't assume that what I asked him to do got him killed. Besides, I've been in touch with the NYPD and they seem to have it under control. They promised to let me know how things are progressing."

"I just feel I should be involved. Get me the password."

"It'll have to wait until morning. My techie is long gone. Is that OK?"

"Sure. Don't forget."

"I won't." Sarah immediately called Alberto. "Alberto, Sorry to bother you so late but I have a problem. My boss wants to get into the account. I don't want to make a big deal of it but I'm afraid that if he sees the file passworded and encrypted he'll blow my cover and fuck up our work. He's such a dodo that I can't trust him with what we're trying to do."

"Dodo, what is a dodo?"

Sarah laughed, "Sorry, a dodo is a dope, dumb."

"Ah, come *l'uccello*, the bird."

"You got it." she answered.

"I have been giving that some thought. How about this? I delete the file and put another file with the same name in its place."

"What could you put in the file?"

"How about the books to be read by the Amerada Book Club in the next twelve months.?"

Sarah laughed. "You're a pistol," she said.

"*Pistole*?"

"Just an expression. Don't take it literally."

"OK. Why don't you text me a list of books? I'll take care of it tonight. Then tomorrow, when you know he's satisfied, I can put the file back with no harm done. Unless of course, one of the bad guys decides to check on things."

"We have to risk it. I'll get him to do it first thing in the morning and finish as fast as I can. Let me get a list together. Check your email."

"I will do that. *Ciao*, Sarah."

Sarah googled the New York Times best seller list and quickly texted a list of ten books to Alberto. Ten minutes later, she got a return text with one word, "Done." She wanted to check to make sure but caught herself. That wouldn't be a good idea. But she could rest easy tonight.

CHAPTER IV

May 10th

Sarah always tried not to take her work home but the thing that worried her as she got into bed was that if these people were monitoring access, would Manson be at risk? Possible, unless of course he was involved, she thought. Knowing Manson, she didn't believe it. Unless of course, he's been acting and playing dumb all these years. She didn't believe that, either. But, she came to the conclusion, better him than me. She knew that Alberto's incursions were not detectable so that wasn't a problem. She wanted to find out where in Arlington this monitoring computer was but didn't know how. She hoped that Alberto would find a way. She dropped off into a deep sleep.

Next morning, her mind began to work again continuing where she left off. Fortunately, she didn't dream about it and enjoyed a good night's sleep. She got to her office early and as she was walking toward the door, she saw Armand walking out. "Looking for something, Armand?"

"Looking to see if you had a local phone book. But I couldn't find one."

"I don't have one," she answered. She took off her coat and sat down.

"I hoped you would."

"Google not good enough for you or switchboard.com?"

"It's someone I'm looking up and I don't know how to spell his name. Just easier for me to use a phone book. But," he smiled, "I guess I'll have to do with Google." He closed the door.

All of a sudden, she began to worry about Armand. Was he nosing around and why? He's been with her for years. She never had any reason to mistrust him. But she was very worried because she didn't know anything. If something was endangering her, she didn't know which direction it was coming from. Trust no one, she thought. Tony was the one who told her what was going on so he wasn't a problem and Alberto certainly was trustworthy. Fortunately, there was nothing for Armand to find. Every communication was via the prepaid telephone which she had in her purse. She checked her purse to make sure.

She called Manson. "Hey, Boss. You ready for what you want to do?"

"Yes I am, Sarah," Manson answered.

"Great, I'll be up in a minute. Armand, I'm going up to twelve. I should be back probably no more than a half hour."

"Very good. Anything special you want me to do?"

"No, not that I can think of." Again, Sarah wondered about Armand. He never volunteered help. This is the second time this week.

"Come in Sarah. Let's do this thing."

"OK, the password is" … she hesitated "Let me do it." she keyed in the password. He was one of those that never really took to using a computer. It was more of a chore than a tool for him.

He was elated. He was into the account and saw the file. "What's in the file?"

"Open it," she said. "Double click on it," she added. She watched while he moved the mouse showing his lack of facility. "Don't you ever use your computer?"

"Sure, I use it a lot but only to check my email."

The file opened and Manson said, "Amerada is a book club? That's what this is about?"

"Now do you believe me?"

"Why don't you just close the account?"

"I'm just hoping that I'll find out who the evil culprit is. The account is not doing anyone any harm. Do us both a favor. Don't try to prove anything to Henry Stafford. He doesn't need to know what you know. Just tell him it's none of his fucking business. Let him stew and wonder."

Manson laughed out loud but Sarah worried and wondered if he wasn't so insecure that he had to show Stafford how smart he was. "I can't let him get away with his pompous attitude."

"Boss, please. Trust me on this. Now you know, so forget about it. You don't need his approval. Tell him what you want but don't make me show him anything. Don't set a precedent where if he asks, you have to prove it. She was almost begging and he was making her sorry she showed him anything. He was such a dunce. She was glad she never gave him the password and wondered just how he got his job. He must have been somebody's crony.

"OK, Sarah. I'll go along with that."

"Talk to you later." She got up and went back to her office. The door was open and she didn't remember if she left it closed. Armand nosing around again she thought. What's with him? She closed the door and texted Alberto. "Done, restore things."

Five minutes later, the answer came. "Restored."

Sarah was relieved. This was the first time in her years at NSA that she was involved in something covert, behaving like an agent. With the pressure there was also a rush that excited her. She wondered if she could ever go back to being a bureaucrat when the Amerada thing was resolved.

Armand stuck his head in. "Going down to get coffee. You want anything?"

"Coffee with milk would be great, thanks. By the way Armand, was anyone in my office while I was upstairs?"

"Not that I know of," he answered. "Why?"

"The door was open."

"You left it open."

She continued to wonder whether Armand was to be trusted. But what could he up to, she wondered? But that would have to go on the back burner. She called Tony and told him what she and Alberto had done.

"You have to watch out now," he said. "I've been thinking about it and if someone is monitoring the account, frustrated as they probably are not able to get to Alberto, they might just get very nasty with your boss."

"I thought about that but, I told you, this place is like a fort."

"But you don't know if someone from NSA is involved or not. If they are, they may already be in the fort."

Sarah thought for a moment. Maybe she should alert the security office. "Let me see what I can do to protect him. Call you later. "

"Bill, Sarah Tepper. Can you drop by my office, second floor? I want to talk about something important"

"Sure Sarah, what's up?"

"I'll tell you when I see you."

"Be there in ten."

"Great, thanks and please not a word to anyone."

Theodore's Apartment

Theodore was very frustrated. He was not used to being thwarted. No matter what he tried, he could not get to the computer that had gotten into the Amerada account. He banged his hand on the desk next to his computer. In addition to his frustration, he was also beginning to get frightened. Herman Flint's threats were not to be taken lightly. He had no protection and he did not trust Flint to keep his word. He had to find that Italian computer.

Just then, his monitoring software beeped at him. Again, he thought? No, this time when he looked, it was another computer that had entered the account. He was able to locate this one easily and decided to take action without asking Flint. He wanted to be aggressive and positive in Flint's eyes, to show him something. He watched while the other computer was looking around the account. After several minutes and the other's logout, his unique search software found the email address of the trespasser. He worked feverishly to set up his specially unique malware and attach it to emails aimed at the trespasser. He sent an email to the address offering sexual massage. Press here to read more. Then, not sure of the sex of the offender, he offered a catalog of beautiful jewelry at a ridiculously low price. Then to make sure of the response, he sent a third email with nothing but a link, saying "You have to see this." When he was done, he watched to make sure the bait was attractive enough and kept his eyes peeled on his monitoring screen.

Milan, Italy

Alberto was working on the Barnhill hard drive. He had succeeded in getting Barnhill's last few emails before his computer exploded. He saw that the one right before he died was a sex solicitation. He laughed. Amazing and predictable, he thought. You want a man's reaction, give him sex. Alberto noticed that the email had a small malware program buried in it. He looked at the code which seemed strange to him. It was simple but strange. He took a short cut. Instead of analyzing it, he keyed it into his computer and executed it. A disturbing hum began immediately. After a few seconds, he touched the screen and it was very hot. The hum increased. An instinctive reaction, he turned off the computer. He decided to analyze it in detail. Shortcuts never work, he thought. He printed out the coded instructions and carefully monitored what they did.

Very clever, he thought to himself and incredibly simple. An infinite loop to overcharge the capacitors in the computer.. Attach it to an email a person cannot resist. If you don't know, try several. An hour later, he called Sarah. "Sarah. This is Alberto. I know how Barnhill was killed."

"How, Alberto?"

"A piece of malware was executed by Barnhill when he answered a sex solicitation. The malware is ingenious. It accesses all the capacitors in the computer and with an infinite program loop, it keeps increasing the charge on all of them at once until they reach a level of overcapacity they can't handle and boom. It blows up."

"That's crazy. The computer blows up? Without warning?"

"There's warning but most people would ignore it. The computer begins to hum and it's a noticeable hum."

"A noticeable hum?"

"Right, this little piece of malware turns the computer into a lethal bomb. And it can be done easily and remotely. All the person has to know is the potential victim's email address, which is easy enough to get and attach it to an irresistible email."

"Thanks, Alberto. Let me go," she said anxiously, "I've got to talk to Bill Armitage about this."

"*Ciao*, Sarah. Good luck and be careful."

Manson's office

Stuart Manson was embarrassed by his ignorance when Sarah came to get him in the Amerada account. After all this time, he knew he was still computer illiterate. Having finally learned how to use his cell phone for more than just a phone, he used his computer even less. With the computer he was as uncomfortable as trying to eat left-handed. He turned on his computer and decided to explore a little. There were so many apps on the screen that he no idea about, he was overwhelmed. Sarah had told him yesterday to just explore. She assured him that he couldn't screw things up. Playing with them would teach him and make him more relaxed about it. She told him not to be ashamed to call her if he needed help.

He usually checked his email on his telephone but he pushed himself past his discomfort and decided to try using the mail app on his computer. He was pleased at the speed the list popped up and the text was large enough that he didn't need his glasses to read anything. That was a real plus he thought. His eyes scanned the list of incoming emails. He laughed at the appeal by a young Russian woman who wanted to meet him. He stopped and opened one that implored him that he had to read this. His curiosity got the best of him.

He called Sarah. "Sarah, I'm on my computer trying to get more familiar with using it. You got me interested with the Amerada thing."

"That's good. It's about time you joined us in the twenty-first century. How's it going?"

"Which apps do you think I should try? There are so many."

"I suggest the first thing you do is get on the internet with the Safari app and google yourself. See what comes up. You might be surprised."

"I tried the mail app and it's great to see things big enough to read. I'm so used to squinting on my telephone screen."

"Don't hesitate to call me if you need help. In fact, I should come up and show you a few things to get you started."

"When?"

She looked at her watch. "You got time now?"

"Sure, come on."

"Be right there. Armand, I'm going up to twelve. If Bill Armitage comes before I'm back, ask him to please wait. I going to twelve."

"Armitage from security? What's up with him?" he asked.

"Can't talk now. Just ask him to wait for me. It's important."

When Sarah entered Manson's office, he was sitting at his computer. As she approached him, she could hear the loud hum Alberto described. "Oh, my God." She rushed up to him, knocked him off his chair and with all her strength dragged them both to the floor face down just as the computer exploded. The loud blast deafened them but the glass from the screen and debris missed them.

"What the... What happened?" he asked.

"You just found out how Barnhill was killed. Fortunately, I found out before you did. That's why I knocked you down."

Sarah called her office. "Armand, is Armitage there?"

"Yes, he just got here."

"Please ask him to come up to twelve, Manson's office as soon as possible."

"Will do. Something wrong?"

"No," she lied, "just send him up here."

Bill Armitage was a big African-American who could easily be mistaken for a former football linebacker, a brawn-only type. It belied his background as a phi beta kappa Northwestern graduate with a law degree from Columbia.

When Armitage arrived, there were three people besides Sarah in Manson's office. They were responding to the explosion. Sarah told them, "Computer defective, it blew up. Fortunately, no one was hurt. We're looking into it. You can go back to your offices. We've got this." She closed the door and asked Bill Armitage to sit. "Listen, Boss, I haven't been truthful with you. I've been worried because I don't know whom to trust. Stafford was a little too interested in this Amerada account. Of all the emails I sent to section heads, telling them it was nothing, to forget it, he was the only one that expressed an interest and what I told him wasn't enough for him. He had to use you to verify that I was no longer interested in the Barnhill killing."

Armitage injected, "I heard about that. Are you involved with that, too?"

"How did you hear?" she asked him.

"Stafford asked me about the account," he replied. "I told him I didn't know anything about it but it couldn't be important."

"You see, Boss, he's got to be involved somehow."

"In what?" Armitage asked.

"I don't know. Something to do with this Amerada account."

"I thought it was nothing. That's what Stafford told me. You sure there's something there?"

"Yes, I engaged a forensic computer expert who has been investigating it for me."

"One of ours?" Manson asked

"No. He was recommended to me by Tony Belvedere, the NYPD forensic guy who knows him well. Claims he's something of a genius."

"But why go outside?" Armitage asked.

"I didn't know whom I could trust. Still don't. It's got to be somebody inside. Otherwise why an NSA locked account that no one knows anything about? The person on it is a Sherlock Holmes type that needs challenges. He told me that there was no way he could be discovered because of how he is set up. And no one knows who or where he is."

Armitage asked, "So how did the computer get bombed?"

"Malware via an email."

"You can't be serious," Armitage replied.

"Oh, I'm very serious. Something very weird is happening and I have to get to the bottom of it. At least now, we know how it's being done. What I don't know is what it's all about. There's a file in the account that's passworded and encrypted."

Manson chimed in, "You mean the Amerada Book Club file."

"Sorry," she looked at Manson. "That was to throw you off the track. Like I said, I didn't know who I could trust."

"You mean you didn't trust me?" Manson said.

"Sorry. Don't take any offense. I didn't trust anybody."

"What about Stafford?" Manson asked.

Sarah answered. "In order to throw everyone off the trail, I let it be known with an email to all the section heads that the Amerada account was a nothing and I no longer had any interest in it. Only Stafford answered."

"What about that book club file? Where did it come from." Manson asked.

"That was a plant to throw you off the trail. The real file is being worked on. There must be information in it that's being sold. And it must be a lot of money if they are killing to protect it."

Armitage asked, "I should look into Stafford, first, don't you think?"

"I looked at his personnel file. He's broke. Used to be rich. I don't know how he lost it all, but he's broke. So he's a candidate. But I'm sure if he is involved, he's not alone. Stafford's not a computer genius. I suspect a group and I don't want to let on or they'll scatter. I want to catch them."

"I agree," Armitage added. "I'll look to see what I can find without giving it away. You'll keep me posted, particularly if you find out what's in the encrypted file?"

"Absolutely, You're involved now whether you like or not. My problem now is how am I going to explain Manson's bomb without giving everything away."

"Let me do that,"Armitage replied, "i"ll say that there was an electrical problem."

"Stafford is going to hear about it and if he's involved, he'll be aware that things are not clear. I'll still somehow indicate that Amerada is not related to this problem. I just don't know if he'll believe it. He'll at least be wary. Also, lately, I don't know if I can trust my assistant, Armand Arnaud."

"Why would you doubt him?" Manson asked.

"Maybe I'm just imagining it but it seems as if he's been nosing around. Also, he's been volunteering himself, something he never did before. Efficient, yes. Accomplishes his tasks but never tries to be nice, that is, until lately."

"Duly noted," Armitage said. "But I doubt he's a problem. He's been with you too long."

CHAPTER V

May 12th

Herman Flint rarely raised his voice but he was irate. "Theodore, are you crazy? Why would you try another bombing without asking? You know we don't want any killing unless it's absolutely necessary. Killing leads to investigation and to possible discovery. You are fortunate, the bomb didn't kill but easily could have. We can't afford that. Is the merchandise still intact?"

"Yes, the file is still there and still encrypted with a password. If someone got the file, it would be impossible to decrypt and pretty useless. So don't worry."

"There is too much as stake for me not to worry. And how someone as smart as you can do such a stupid thing, I can't imagine. Have you found the Italian trespasser yet?"

"No, and it has not entered the account for three days now. So maybe it was just a mistake or a rogue hacker trolling. But there would be nothing for a stranger to see. That might explain why there's no more attempts by the Italian."

"I hope you are right. Keep me posted and don't take matters into your own hands. I still would like to know what Italian is looking into the account and why. Maybe you are wrong. We have to be sure."

"I'll keep after it, Mr. Flint."

Flint shook his head and left Theodore. He immediately made a phone call. "Just stupid. I know, I know. I'll keep him under control. OK."

Sarah's office

"It's pretty clear now, Tony," Sarah said. "The killings are almost certainly related and when we find out who's involved, you'll know who killed Barnhill."

"What happened at NSA?"

"Alberto, bless him, figured out how the computer was bombed." She then explained to Tony what Alberto told her about the malware. "Apparently, my boss entering the Amerada account prompted a bomb attempt just as Alberto described it to me. As luck would have it, I got there just in time so no one was hurt. But, boy it was close. Could have killed two of us."

"Wow. Please be careful, Sarah. I'd hate to lose you before I even get to know you."

"You mean know me in the biblical sense?"

Tony laughed, "That, too. But I'm trying not to be so obvious."

She chuckled. "I'll be careful. I just hope Alberto succeeds in decrypting the Amerada file, and sooner rather than later. The longer it takes, the less likely we are to find out who or what. Whoever is doing this is, I'm sure, in the middle of a negotiation. So there's a time limit and we don't know what it is."

"You're probably right on. Keep alert, Mi raccomando. Talk soon."

"Bye, Tony"

Sarah called Bill Armitage. "Bill, is it possible to get a record of calls made from Armand Arnaud's telephone. He hasn't done anything but he's just too nice, out of character. Maybe I'm paranoid, but I don't know who I can trust."

"Sure. We have those records and keep them as good security administration.. But if he uses his own cell phone, we're not out of luck but it's more difficult.."

"Unless I can look at his cell phone, right?"

"True, but be careful. Wait until I get the records together. He might have been careless."

"OK, I'll wait. How soon will you have them?"

"This afternoon but you better come get them yourself. I don't want them to pass Arnaud's desk You never know."

"What time?"

"Anytime after say two."

"Great, bye" Sarah slumped back into her chair. Not much to do now but wait.

Yuri's problem

"Valery, it's Yuri. What do you think about solving my problem?"

"Well, it's a difficult task, Yuri. Getting into the account is not so difficult. I don't know what I will find in the account. I'm sure it's not just sitting there waiting to be hacked."

"What could you find?"

"The information would likely be difficult to access, like encrypted or with a password. They are not fools."

"If it is encrypted, what does that take?"

"Getting the information from an encrypted file or files, is not an easy task, and if it's an NSA file, the encryption would probably be 64 bit and very difficult to break, if not almost impossible."

"Valery, my friend, I thought you were an expert."

"I am an expert, Yuri, but not a magician. I can try but I cannot guarantee anything."

"I will give you ten thousand American dollars for a serious attempt. If you succeed within a few days, the fee will be five million, also American dollars."

"You are joking Yuri?"

"No, I am not. That's what it's worth. Will you try?"

"Of course, for that kind of money. But as I said before, I cannot guarantee anything."

"Fine, I will send the ten thousand by courier in an hour. Please begin as soon as you receive the cash."

"I will certainly try."

"Call me if you have any questions, Valery. Remember, five million if you succeed. But time is short. You have no more than six days."

"Very difficult, particularly in six days but hard to ignore the incentive, Yuri. Very hard," he laughed.

As he hung up the phone, Yuri turned to his companion, "Andrei, it is worth a try. A ten thousand dollar investment to save three hundred million? Definitely worth the risk."

"Don't you think you might give us away if you do?"

"I have already got the money approved but I will stall them. I want to try this before I turn over three hundred. It's possible I will be discovered, Andrei, but still worth trying. If it doesn't work, we will still make the transaction. They won't refuse. But, three hundred million is a lot of money."

"But Yuri, it's not our money. Why risk it?"

"It just annoys me for our agency to pay so much when, with a small investment, we can get it anyway." Yuri checked the money in the briefcase and called his courier. "Here is the package to deliver. Get me a signed receipt, please." He handed the courier the briefcase and the address scribbled on a piece of paper."

"Yes sir. I shall go now."

"I hope everything works out, Yuri. But I still think you are taking an unnecessary risk. We want that information very badly. Three hundred million sounds like a lot of money but for the government, it's not."

Yuri shrugged. "If three hundred million is small, ten thousand is coffee money. We'll see, we'll see."

Sarah's office

Sarah pored over the phone list she got from Armitage. Almost all the calls were numbers she recognized. There were a few too many unfamiliar cell phones, a couple were repeated several times. Armitage had to trace them. She scanned the list and saved it on her computer with a weird unrelated file name and password to keep snoopers away. Then she wrote down the numbers of the unfamiliar cell phones for Armitage, and shredded the list of calls.

She texted Armitage with the numbers she wanted him to run down and then shredded the sheet of paper. Being extra careful, she also erased the text message she just sent. Sarah picked up the ringing office telephone. It was Manson.

"Sarah, Stafford just called me. I thought you should know."

"What did he say?" she asked anxiously.

"He asked what happened. He heard my computer blew up."

"What did you tell him?"

"I told him what we agreed. That it was an electrical problem. And since I'm not a rocket scientist, I told him to call Armitage who diagnosed the problem."

"How did he react to the answer?"

"Couldn't tell."

Sarah was becoming very concerned. Stafford was no dummy. If he was so curious and inserted himself into the loop, he must be involved somehow. He must also be aware of the exploding computer syndrome. Up to now they've been ruthless and murdered indiscriminately. Stafford knows Manson a long time and must know he's not very bright. But, then Sarah got scared, he must also know she was no dope and has only been pretending a lack of interest. She planned to keep pretending and make Stafford doubt himself.

He couldn't take action against her unless he was sure. There had been too many fatal and near-fatal incidents. Stafford didn't know who was aware of Amerada. If anything happened to Sarah unnecessarily, the whole deal would blow up. Sarah thought if she succeeded in pretending, he would keep pushing to find out what she knew and perhaps give himself away. Stafford was also worried that Theodore was a loose cannon and would bring the whole deal down with his impulsiveness.

Armand opened Sarah's door and looked in. "I'm leaving for the day. Is there anything before I go?"

"I can't think of anything. See you tomorrow."

After he closed the door she pondered his behavior. He never was so considerate she thought. Is he involved in this thing? It was after 7 p.m. when Sarah left and went to the garage. The two men surprised her when she got to her car. One opened the car door, grabbed her, pulled her out and held her while the other put a black hood over her head. She screamed as she was pushed back into the back seat of her car and he got in after her. Her screams were muffled by the hood.

The driver rifled through her purse to find the car keys then started the engine and drove to the garage exit. When they got to the exit gate, there was a car blocking the exit. They honked the horn. The driver of the blocking car got out and walked up to the car. The driver opened the window partially. The man from the blocking car said. "Sorry, I'm stuck. Can you give me a hand so I can get out of your way?"

"What's the problem?" the driver asked. The other man had his hand over Sarah's mouth with the hood still on.

"Engine died on me. I can't get it started. I'm a car dummy. Maybe you can help me get it started."

The driver got out of the car and just as he did, the other man gave him a knee to the groin and a chop across the neck which knocked him out. He quickly opened the back door and pulled the other man out simultaneously giving him a hard blow to the solar plexus which knocked him down. He then pulled Sarah out and removed the hood. The two men were still down but moaning.

"Armand. What are you doing here?"

"I have been concerned since the Amerada thing. Your behavior was much too mysterious. I decided to pay a bit more attention to what is going on. When I got to the garage to leave, I saw the two men waiting near your car so I decided to wait around and see if things were all right."

Both men got up and ran off. Armand ran after them but they got into a waiting elevator and the door closed after them. Armand looked up to see what floor they were going to. It was the lobby so he went back to Sarah who was watching.

"I can't thank you enough, Armand."

"I'm sorry they got away. I wanted to find out who sent them. Meanwhile, you should go home. I will follow you in my car to make sure no one is waiting for you at your apartment."

When Sarah got home, she called Armand to tell him she was in the apartment and was fine. Only then did Armand leave. This affair gave Sarah much to think about. Who grabbed her and why? And how could she be so wrong about Armand?

Chapter VI

May 13th

The next morning on her way to the office, Sarah felt better that she was wrong about Armand, but still decided to keep her own counsel. The fewer people who knew what was going on the better. But at least, she wasn't so tense with him around. He appeared to have her safety at heart and she had misjudged him.

"Good morning, Sarah," Armand spoke as if nothing was out of the ordinary. When she went into her office, Armand followed her. He closed the door and said, "Sarah, do you know what that was all about last evening?"

"No, Armand. I don't. And let me thank you again."

"You have no idea?" he added.

"Not even a hint," she lied.

"Shouldn't we call the police or tell someone about this?"

"What are we going to tell them?" Sarah said, as if asking for an idea. "They have nothing to go on to find out anything. There's nothing they can do. Protect me? Not likely. But there is something I can do to even the odds." She opened the bottom drawer of her desk and took a Ruger LC9 pistol she hadn't touched in years. She pulled out a magazine, snapped it into the handle and pointed it. "I think I'll go to the range and get myself comfortable with it again."

Armand winced. "When did you get that?"

"About four years ago. For some silly reason I thought I should have a handgun. But until now, I really had no need for it." She put the pistol and an extra loaded magazine in her purse and dialed the gun range to make an appointment.

"I'm going down for coffee. You want some?" He asked.

"I could use one, thanks." She got increasingly curious about what could be in the encrypted file in the Amerada account. What could be so valuable and to whom? The only thing she could think of was information our enemies might use. Russia? Iran? China? North Korea? But what kind of information would be worth so much as to result in killings? The NSA doesn't have any weapons information. Personnel data? But what could be worth big money? She decided to stop at Armitage's office on the way to the gun range.

"Hey, Sarah. Come on in," Armitage gave her a hand signal.

"Hi, Bill. Just stopped by to see if you uncovered any of our mysteries."

"I've been tracking Arnaud's numbers and nothing on them is suspicious. I also got information from his cell phone and even those calls were benign."

"He could have another cell phone."

"True, but let's not be paranoid."

"So you think he's clean?"

"I didn't say that. So far, I haven't found anything."

Sarah volunteered, "I wanted to tell you something. Last night I was assaulted in the garage going to my car. Armand rescued me but the men got away."

"What happened?"

"One guy grabbed me and put a hood over my head and pushed me into the back seat. The other started my car and started to drive. Armand's car apparently blocked the way. I don't know exactly what happened because I was crouched in the back with a hood over my head. After I heard a tussle, Armand reached in and pulled me out and took the hood off me. Two men were down next to the car but as Armand checked to see if I was all right, the men suddenly got up and ran.

"When was that?"

"It happened about 7:30," she answered.

"What was he doing there? That's a little strange."

"He left sometime before me and claimed that he saw the men waiting near my car and decided to wait and see. He said he's been worried about me."

"Why should he be worried about you?"

"He said that lately he thinks I've been stressed in some way."

"Sounds reasonable. Maybe he really is watching out for you."

"I still don't want to tell him what's going on. The fewer the better."

"I agree," he said. "I'm looking into Stafford and Manson now."

"Manson? Why Manson?"

"If I'm gonna check, I'll check everything. Then I can eliminate what's not significant. This is NSA, remember? We are the ultimate checkers," he laughed.

"How can I forget? Especially now that I'm no longer a desk jockey. I'm on my way to the gun range. I decided to take my pistol out of mothballs."

"Not a bad idea. The NRA would be excited. I'll keep you posted. Meanwhile, don't forget, aim for the target."

"Thanks for the advice. See you later."

****

At the gun range, it didn't take long for Sarah to familiarize herself with the gun again. By the second go round, she was hitting the target in or very near the bull's eye.

When Sarah got back to her office that afternoon, she had a voice mail message from Armitage. Armand was not at his desk. She called Armitage right away.

"Bill, Sarah. What's up?

"I've been checking Stafford and Manson. First of all, it appears that Manson is clean. His whole history of phone messages and everything else about him is benign. Stafford on the other hand is a bit more mysterious. Some of his appointments and phone calls are a little out of mainstream procedure. It's as if he's moonlighting. It's just hard to connect the dots. But I'll keep working on it.

"What about Armand?"

"Armand is also clean on his phone, even his cell. In fact, it's too clean as if he's being careful. It's as if a burglar keeps wiping fingerprints clean. I'm willing to bet he has another cell phone. But I'll keep on with him and Stafford and let you know."

"Nothing in writing, please. And no one else but me."

"Oh, that's understood. Talk to you later."

As soon as she hung up, Armand walked into her office. "Hi Sarah. You OK?"

"Why shouldn't I be?" she looked up and asked him.

"After last night. You still have no idea who those people were and what that was about?"

"Not the slightest."

"You're not going to tell me what's been bothering you the last few days?"

She smiled, "It's a little personal and really not something I want to discuss, least of all with you, nice as you are. I'm sure what happened last night had no relation to my personal problem. That would be a real stretch."

"Sorry for sticking my nose in," he said. "You can imagine that I'm curious about who those guys were."

"So am I. And if I find out, I'll tell you. But for now, I haven't got the slightest idea who or why. And I haven't got the time to waste to track them. I'm still trying to find out about Conaghey's mugging death in New York and Barnhill's death."

"Anything new on that?"

"Not a fucking thing." She used the word for emphasis, to show Armand her displeasure. She was not prone to use profanity. "Unfortunately it's the New York police that are working on it. If they find out anything, they'll call me. I'm a little frustrated."

"What about the Amerada thing?" he asked.

"Oh, that. That's a nothing. It's not hurting anyone so I'll let it go for the time being. When I get some time, I'll find out whose it is. What's your interest in it?"

"None, just curiosity. I hear things."

"What things?"

"Nothing much except there's an account that no one knows anything about."

"True but I'm sure it's a nothing, Still, no one is owning up to owning it. I have no time to chase it down now. Gotta work. Anything else?"

"No, I'll leave you alone." He left and closed the door.

Sarah got up and cracked open her door to see if Armand was making any phone calls. He was poring over papers on his desk. She closed the door and sat down and rocked herself in her chair thinking what she could do next. Maybe Armand really was looking out for her. She called Tony Belvedere.

"Tony, Sarah."

"Hi, this is a pleasant surprise, You've made my day."

"Ha. Flattery get's you nowhere. I would like you to do me a favor and call our friend for status. I don't want to call him from here. Can you do that for me?"

"Would be my pleasure. Tell me, what are you doing this weekend? You got any plans?" he asked.

"Nothing special. Laundry, I suppose."

"Why don't you meet me for dinner Saturday, say in Philadelphia. It's halfway."

"That's an interesting idea. I'd like that if we make it early so I don't have to drive back too late."

"How about five? That early enough?"

"That works. Where should we meet?"

"I'd like to try The Rose Tattoo Cafe on Callow Hill Street. I've heard great things about it. Put it in your GPS."

"It's a date. Meanwhile, you'll call our friend?"

"I certainly will. Talk to you later."

"Don't call me about that. We can talk about it on Saturday, OK? Unless it's earth-shattering. "

"That's fine. See you then."

Theodore's apartment

Theodore called Flint and when he answered, Theodore nervously said, "Mr. Flint, there is someone in Moscow who is trying to get into the Amerada site."

"Moscow? Are you sure?"

"Yes, I'm sure. But I can't identify him."

"Has he succeeded?"

"I don't believe he has. But he is definitely not a mistake. He has been trying continuously for two days now."

"Why didn't you call me sooner?" Flint said angrily.

"I wanted to make sure it wasn't an accident. I'm sure now it's not."

Flint replied after a few seconds of silence. "Is there any way to find out who it is?"

"I'll try but it's difficult. I can get his email address but I don't have the tools to find out who had that email address."

"OK, I'll get back to you. Is your weapon still functioning?"

"As far as I know it is."

"OK, Wait for my call."

Flint walked out of Theodore's earshot and made a call. When the answer came, Flint said, "There is someone in Russia trying to get into Amerada. Theodore cannot tell who it is."

"Can he tell where in Moscow"? The phone voice asked.

Flint turned to Theodore, "Can you tell where in Moscow the person is?"

Theodore answered. "No. I can try to find out but it's difficult to pinpoint."

"He can try to find out... OK. Theodore, see if you can get us a little closer than Moscow."

"I will try and call you."

"Thank you," Flint said. "It's very important." He put on his hat and left the apartment.

Theodore sat at his computer. He felt a little better for the moment, since he had provided information and Flint wasn't angry at him. He was able to see clearly that someone in Moscow was trying to enter Amerada. It wasn't like the Italian that he could not see and who stopped trying. The Moscow person was fighting hard to get into the account but without success. Theodore used every hacking tool he had to get into the intruder's computer without success. He was getting more frustrated and with the passage of time, his frustration was turning to fear. He was not secure with Mr. Flint who had already threatened him with finding another tech to work with them. Theodore had a lot invested in time for the money that was promised to him.

He called Flint. "Mr. Flint, this is Theodore. I cannot determine where the intruder is. I have tried to hack into his computer without success. So it is impossible for me to locate him precisely."

"I'm sorry to hear that, Theodore. Is there anything else you can tell me other than that he is in Moscow?"

"The only thing so far is that he continues to try feverishly to get into the account but has not had any success yet."

"How about the Italian?" Flint asked.

"No further activity from him. I think that was an accident. In my opinion it is nothing to worry about."

"Thank you Theodore. I would like you to keep trying."

"I will, Mr. Flint." He hung up and was somewhat relieved but still felt that his life was under threat if he did not succeed. He went back to his computer and got himself focused.

The voice on the phone said to Stafford, "Henry, based on Theodore's information, I strongly suspect that we are being played by our customer."

"What do you mean, played?"

"I would like to verify it but I suspect that our customer is trying to save himself millions by stealing what he is committed to buy from us."

Stafford answered, "You can't possibly believe that. Why would he do that? It's not his money and we know the purchase has been approved."

"That's true," the voice said. "But I suspect he would like very much that the money becomes his and he sees a way. It's pretty transparent. The only doubt is whether it is truly our customer that is involved and not another party."

"What do you have in mind?"

"I will let you know," the voice hung up abruptly.

CHAPTER VII

Saturday Afternoon.

Sarah took her laundry out of the dryer. She had made up her mind that date or no date, she would do her laundry. She folded everything and carefully put it all away and jumped into the shower to get ready for her date with Tony. She was excited. Since she broke up with Elliot, years earlier, she buried herself in her work. At first it was therapy but by now it had evolved into habit, and not a good one. She never realized how time was passing and how one dimensional her life had become until she met and was attracted to Tony Belvedere. She needed a half hour to primp, make sure she looked her best and got into her car.

Less than two hours later, she pulled up to the restaurant and looked at her watch. She had time to look for a parking lot. After a short drive around the block, she found one and dropped off the keys with the parking attendant. "I'll be about two hours. Please don't bury it."

The attendant gave her a ticket and smiled, "It'll be right here," he said pointing to a space very nearby.

"Thanks," she answered, putting the ticket in her handbag. When she entered the restaurant, she immediately saw Tony waving at her. She walked past the maitre d' right to the table. He got up and gave her a peck on the cheek.

"How was your trip?" he asked. "Mine was fast but I hate the New Jersey Turnpike."

"My ride was pretty good. You here long?"

"Only a few minutes."

"Can we get a bottle of red wine and stretch it over the meal?" she asked. "I hate to drive back with a buzz."

He called the waiter over and pointed to a Chianti Classico on the wine menu. "Very good," the waiter quickly disappeared.

"While we're waiting," she said, "can we get our business out of the way. Did you talk to Alberto?"

"Yes, I did. He apparently is now able to monitor intrusions into the Amerada account. He has not decoded the Amerada file yet but thinks he is making progress. He has discovered that in addition to the Arlington person who he presumes is the owner of the account or working for the owner, there has been just in the last two days someone making a furious effort to get into the account."

"Wow. I wonder who that is."

"Not only that, the person is in Moscow."

"Double wow," she answered.

"Alberto and I both came to the same conclusion – that the Moscow person is probably their customer for whatever Amerada has to sell."

"But why would he be trying to get into the account frantically?" she asked.

"Don't know. I could speculate, but that's not what you need."

"Try me."

"Someone is trying to steal what's in the account," he answered.

Sarah thought for a moment as the waiter was pouring the wine for Tony to taste. He nodded his head and the waiter filled their glasses. "How would someone know what's in the account or even what the account name is?" she asked.

"Someone who has good intel. Sounds like you've got a mole feeding information to the intruder. It could be the customer, or a thief who is aware of the value."

Sarah thought for a minute. "Sounds to me like someone is playing both sides," she answered. "Otherwise it doesn't make any sense."

The waiter took their order. She ordered a house salad and frenched breast of chicken. He ordered spicy clams and baby back ribs. "Very good," the waiter said.

"If someone is trying to steal it, it could be the customer who doesn't want to pay for it, or a competitive buyer who also wants whatever it is and has been refused by the seller," she said.

"Both of those make some sense. Have you any ideas about any of the interested players? You're closer to it than I am."

"Henry Stafford is definitely a suspect. I thought my assistant might be involved but he saved me from assailants the other night. So I sort of acquitted him, at least for now."

"How about your boss? Manson, right?"

"Too dumb. I've been working for him for quite a few years. I don't believe his denseness is an act. Besides, he almost got himself blown up, remember? Damned if I know what to do next."

"I think you should play it passively and wait to see how Alberto does. If you find out what's in the file, you might get a better idea who is behind it."

Sarah thought for a moment. "You're probably right. Right now, I'm flying blind."

"Also, being passive takes the pressure off the guilty to eliminate you as a threat."

"I'm worried that this deal is imminent and we don't know what's being given and to whom. I wouldn't want to fail in stopping whatever it is," she said, with a frown.

"You can delay it, if you don't know enough to stop it," he answered.

"How?"

"We can tell Alberto to erase the file and substitute it with something innocuous. After all, he has a copy of it. Then when the buyer finds out it's garbage, there is likely to be all kinds of reaction. That would take time to resolve or replace the file. It might even generate the kind of activity that would expose what's happening."

She reacted instantly. "That sounds like a great idea. But it would have to be something that looks real. Not the Times best sellers." She handed him her private phone. "Call him to do that."

"Now?"

"Sure, why not? We don't know when the deal is going to be consummated. I'll feel better if I know the sale won't be made."

Alberto answered his phone. "*Pronto.*"

"What are you doing up so late? I just expected to leave you a voice mail."

"Ah, Tony. Just in case you think I am not working on this *dannato* file. *Mi fa impazzire* and that's why I'm still awake."

"I'm here with Sarah. We think that if a deal to sell it's contents is imminent, it's better if we prevent or delay that by erasing the file and substituting something useless."

"I was thinking the same thing. What I have discovered is that the file contains very little text. Most of the content is computer code, encrypted, but still computer code. I'm almost positive that they are selling computer programs."

"Then you should definitely erase the file and substitute something," he said.

"Consider it done. I can substitute a bunch of commonly known malware programs and leave the file unencrypted."

"Thanks and get some sleep. Keep us posted on your progress."

"Ciao, amico mio. I miei migliori saluti alla Sarah."

"Lo faro'. Ciao.

"He sends you his best. He had the same idea. He'll do it now, substituting some well known malware. He said the file is mostly computer code."

"Computer code? Now it's beginning to make sense," she said. "The NSA is loaded with incredibly powerful hacking tools. They're worth a fortune on the open market," she said. "Someone who has access to them limits my list of suspects."

"Let's finish our dinner and go for a walk. It's a nice evening and we have some time before it gets too late to drive."

"Good idea. I've got all day tomorrow to think about this."

They walked casually, talking about everything from music to Italy. There was chemistry between them and they both felt it. When it seemed the right time for Sarah to leave, they had trouble saying their goodbyes. Their goodbye kiss was a serious thing and they looked each other other in the eyes as Sarah started the engine. The only thing Tony could say was "drive carefully and call me when you get home." Sarah said nothing.

CHAPTER VIII

May 17th

Theodore called from his cell phone. "Mr. Flint, the Italian has briefly accessed the account again but the Moscow intruder is still frantically trying to get into the account. He has been trying continually for days now.

"Has the Russian succeeded?"

"Not that I can see. The Italian, I don't know because his activity is completely blocked but his attempt was very brief, too brief to be significant."

"Thank you, Theodore."

The buyer

"Yuri?"

"Yes, Who is this?"

"You know who this is. I want to inform you that our deal is off. We will be going to the other customer."

"What? You can't do that."

"Yes I can and I will. I can say it was not a pleasure dealing with you."

"What's wrong? What happened?"

"We have reason to believe that you are trying to enter our account. You have no reason to do that unless you are doing something illicit."

"I admit that but I was only trying to verify that we are getting value. Three hundred million is a lot of money."

"I told you exactly what you are getting. There is no reason to do what you are doing."

"OK. I apologize. Please, you must reconsider."

There was silence on the phone for almost a minute. Then the answer came. "One more chance. But you must cease all attempts to enter the account or the deal is off and there will be other serious consequences."

"OK, OK, agreed."

"When will we consummate the sale?"

"Next week."

"Tell me the truth. Are you delaying in order to continue hacking into our account? If you have the money approved, why the delay?"

"No, the delay is arranging cash in dollars, which takes time to do it in an untraceable way. We cannot have the transaction detected."

"All right. I will expect to hear from you next week. Tell me, I can arrange a Swiss account to transfer the money to. The cash can be a bit of a headache."

"I'll let you know." The phone clicked the disconnect.

Yuri and Stafford

"Henry, can you get the password? We have no more time to keep trying."

Stafford answered hesitatingly, "I can, Yuri, but there are two problems with that. First, I can get it but I have no reason to have it. I don't have any reason to even be discussing it. So if I ask for it, there is serious danger that it will blow things open. Secondly, it won't do you any good because the file is encrypted and I cannot get the encryption password. You have to keep trying."

"I can't. Time is gone. He actually cancelled the deal. I made up a story about why we were doing it and convinced him to give me another chance. But I'm sure he is very wary."

"My suggestion would be to try until time is up and then, if we are not successful, pay the money. But they are obviously monitoring the account and have a weapon that can kill remotely. So be very careful. If we pay, our take will still be sizable. Not as much as if we succeed in stealing the file but certainly enough. Greed can kill us. So tell Valery to be careful."

"OK, I will tell Valery to continue but that, too, is risky. If they are monitoring the account, they will know that we are still working on it and that could cost us the deal. We know he has another customer. I will try one more day. No more. I can explain one day to him as an administrative delay, but he will not believe me if there are more. But I am not very optimistic because he has not even gotten into the account, let alone decrypt the file which is much more difficult. One day, then we stop and pay the money."

Flint called Theodore, "This is Flint. Please continue to monitor the account and if the Russian continues the intrusions, you have my instruction to eliminate him."

"All right, Mr. Flint." Theodore went back to his computer and looked at the screen, typing a few words. Then he went to his refrigerator for some yogurt and to the kitchen drawer for a spoon.

Sarah's Office, that same morning.

"How was your weekend?" Armand asked. "Weather finally turned nice."

"True, it was nice. Unfortunately, I was overloaded with laundry to do."

"Couldn't have taken you the whole weekend? You've got to get a life Sarah."

Sarah was puzzled but went along with him. Why does Armand suddenly care about her life, she asked herself. He never cared before, not even a whit. "Well, I have to admit, I did drive to Philly to have dinner with a friend."

"That's good to hear," he replied. "Anyone special?"

"Just an old friend that I haven't seen since my college days. It was very pleasant. I didn't get back in town too late."

"I'm going to get some coffee. Can I get you something?"

"No, thanks, Armand. I'll go out for about an hour but I'll wait till you come back." When he left, Sarah called Armitage. "Bill, are you available? I'd like to talk to you."

"Sure, when?"

"In about a half hour. That OK?"

"Fine. See you then."

Sarah entered Bill Armitage's office and closed the door. She tried to do it casually so as not to hint at anything out of the ordinary. "Anything interesting since we last spoke?"

"I'm sure your boss is clean as far as Amerada is concerned. Stafford is not. Some of his contacts have been to an unknown number repeatedly. I have the information on the phone but it's no help."

"Why not?" she asked. "Whose number is it?"

"It's in the name of a Lieutenant Alexander Kije."

"Who is he?"

"Lieutenant Kije was a fictional officer in the Tsar's army. He was invented by accident and got promoted continuously until the Tsar wanted to meet him. Naturally, he couldn't be found."

"Ah, that's the character Prokofiev made famous. It was used in the movie *The Horses's Mouth*, an Alec Guinness classic."

I have been trying to find out who this one really is but no luck so far. What have you been doing?"

"We have not broken the encryption on the file but we have deduced from the raw encrypted data that most of the content is computer code. There is very little text."

Armitage's eyes lit up. "Now that makes sense."

"My sentiments exactly."

"We have a pot full of incredibly sophisticated computer hacking tools that our enemies would pay a lot of money for."

"That's why I've had the file removed from the account and substituted it with innocuous malware, something well known and deciphered. I got worried that if a deal is imminent, I want to be sure it fails, that there won't be anything to sell."

"Good idea. That also gives me some focus as to where to look for answers. I can do some searching about what, if any, software has been pilfered or asked about, requested and so on and who did it. There has got to be a trail somewhere."

"OK, keep me posted. I'll get back to you if I hear anything new." She got up, waved a goodbye and left, smiling at the secretary as she passed her desk. When she got back to her office, Armand told her that there was a message from the New York police.

"They said they wanted to ask you some questions about the mugging case they were working on."

"Must be the Conaghey case. Did they say anything else?"

"No. Just to call NYPD. He said you would know who."

"I wish I did know who," she lied. "Did they leave a number?"

"Yes. I left it on your desk."

"Thanks." When Sarah looked at the number it wasn't familiar. She dialed it and the answer was, "New York Police Department, may I direct your call?" Sarah knew it was Tony who did not want to leave his name or extension.

"That's a big help," she said. "Did he – it was a he, no? - leave a name or number?"

"No. Strange that he didn't leave his name. But he did say he would call again."

"Thanks Armand. I'm not going to worry about it. If it's important, they'll call back."

"I'm going out for a bite." he said.

"Leave the door open." She wanted to see Armand leave before she called Tony. She didn't know why but she still felt uncomfortable with Armand. It was an instinct. His personality had changed too much. He had become too nice. But he did save her from those two men. She decided that until she knew what was going on, nobody was to be trusted. There was Tony, Bill Armitage and of course Alberto. That's all. When she saw Armand leave, she took out her anonymous phone and called Tony. "You looking for me?"

"Ah Sarah. I texted your special phone and there was no response so I tried your office. I didn't leave any information."

She looked down at her phone but didn't see any message. But just as she was ready to tell Tony that she didn't get it, it flashed on the screen. "Just got it. Alberto called you?"

"Yes. He said that there was frantic intrusion trying to get into the account for about three hours, then it stopped suddenly. He didn't know what it meant but thought he should mention it."

"Thanks, Tony. I'll see if there's any reaction on this end and call you tonight."

"Looking forward to it. Please be careful. My gut tells me that things are not happening for our thieves according to plan. That usually worries me because the future becomes totally unpredictable."

"I'll watch it. If you talk to Alberto again. Call me."

"Will do. Take care."

CHAPTER IX

Later that afternoon, Moscow

Valery had a sense of urgency now. Yuri had ordered him to stop trying with the Amerada account. Yuri had made excuses to the seller and promised to stop. But there was ten million U.S. dollars waiting for Valery if he could get into the account and decrypt the file. He was not willing to give up so easily. Yuri will never know, he told himself. Another day or two couldn't hurt. He felt he was so close. He took a sip of his coffee and decided to check his beeping mail program. When he read the offer of his choice of local nymphomaniacs, he began to laugh. The email was so amusing to him, he didn't notice the hum building up behind his computer screen.

Yuri called Stafford, "Henry, bad news."

"Yuri, what happened?" Stafford asked anxiously.

"Valery is in the hospital. He was critically injured."

"My god, what happened?"

"His computer blew up in his face."

"Just like what happened here. How bad is it?" Stafford was getting worried.

"He is in surgery. I don't know how bad it is."

"I hope it didn't jeopardize the deal. Have you heard anything?"

"No. I'll just assume everything is OK and explain that he was instructed in no uncertain terms to stop, but his curiosity and the challenge wouldn't let him. But for sure, we will pay the cash. I will call him and tell him we can consummate the transaction right away because the cash has been arranged," Yuri said.

"Good, the sooner the better. I'm getting worried that our identities will be discovered before we can settle."

"But you said that this Sarah person thinks it's all nothing."

"That's what she says. Her boss also says so. My nose tells me otherwise. I don't believe she really thinks that. She hasn't got the experience, granted, but she's too smart to let it go. I think she is continuing to investigate surreptitiously. I want to get out of here as soon as I can. I can hear the footsteps, so to speak. It's beginning to worry me."

"OK. Let's try to get it done right away."

Yuri paced back and forth waiting for the phone call. He had just talked to the doctor at the hospital. Valery was out of surgery and in critical condition but the doctor was encouraged and felt that Valery, being young and healthy, would survive. He would need plastic surgery to repair the damaged face but would pull through. Yuri was partly relieved and anxious because he did not know what had happened. The unknown always worried him. Finally, the phone rang. "Hello."

"I am sorry for the injury to your friend," the voice said. "I warned you that if you did not stop there would be serious repercussions. What happened? Why didn't you stop as you promised?"

"I ordered my tech person to stop but the incentive I gave him was too big and he was reluctant to cease his efforts. I, too, am sorry. But now, I want to settle this as soon as possible.

'Transfer the money to the account I will text to you. I will bring the merchandise on two copies of a DVD. Bring a computer so you can check to be sure of what you are getting."

Yuri looked down at the text message that just came in. Yuri answered. "I have just received your text. I will see you tomorrow morning." He hung up without another word.

CHAPTER X

May 18th

The white van pulled up in front of a warehouse. As it approached, the entrance door opened up and a man signaled Yuri to drive in. The door closed after him. When he got out of the truck, he noticed two men with rifles on a mezzanine walkway overlooking the main floor. Yuri and Andrei were there and unarmed. Andrei was a little edgy but Yuri was not worried. His government was relentless in tracking down and killing those that double-crossed them. The seller was well aware of that too, so Yuri didn't give it much thought. The man handed Yuri an envelope.

Yuri took the disk and as he put it in the computer DVD reader, the man said, "The password is Pneumonia666, with a capital P You'll need it to decrypt the file."

"But the file is not encrypted," Yuri said.

"What? Let me see," he said in a quiet panic. Yuri showed him the screen. There were separate sets of computer code readily available without a password. "That is not the merchandise you bought. I will contact you as soon as I find out what is happening." Without another word, he got into his car and sped off.

"What was that all about?" Andrei asked him.

"I don't know. Someone has beaten us to the merchandise and substituted it with shit. I hope the damage is not irreparable."

"What do you mean?"

"I mean, I hope he can find the missing merchandise. He will contact me as soon as he can. We have transferred the cash so he knows we are not fooling. Let's get out of here." They looked at the gunmen overlooking them who were just waiting for them to leave.

Flint answered his phone. "Herman, the merchandise has been stolen from the Amerada account. The only person that could possibly have done it is Sarah Tepper. Unless you think Theodore had something to do with it."

"I doubt that. It's not in his temperament. Besides, he does not have the password for the file so it would not do him any good. He knows his payday is based on a concluded deal," Herman answered.

"I suspect that if she didn't do it, she at least had something to do with it. I don't think she is as innocent as she is pretending. I want you to send out two or three men to get her. You know where to bring her. Wait until she leaves this evening. I don't want her to be missed until tomorrow.

Make sure she is hooded so that she does not know where she is going and see that she remains hooded and is tied up until I get there. She must not be able to identify me. And see to it that nothing happens to her. Is that clear?"

"Yes, I will take care of it."

Sarah's office

Sarah answered the call from Alberto. She looked to see if anyone was eavesdropping outside her office. Armand had called to say he would be a little late. "Hello, Alberto. What's happening?"

"I called you, Sarah, because things are rather urgent now. As I told you, the intrusion stopped. I don't know why. But last evening, the false file I put in the account was downloaded by someone and erased from the account."

"That's could be trouble, but in a sense it's OK. Things must be coming to a head. Maybe we can finally solve this thing."

"I can only assume the transaction has been done or will be done very soon. If that's the case, they will realize that the real file has been removed. Is there anyone other than you that the culprits might suspect?"

"I don't know."

"Then you best be very careful. I expect they will be frantic to get the file back. They didn't want it to be discovered at NSA so they erased the file after they made a copy for delivery. Now they have to find out where the original is."

"I don't really think I'm in any danger," she said casually.

"Sarah, you are badly mistaken. If I am right you are in serious danger. They must assume that you know where the file is and they will stop at nothing to get it. They have already killed at least twice. I believe that what was being sold was extremely valuable and the money was very large because it could only be a government that is the customer. Put that together with the intrusions into the account from Moscow and, as we say, *due più due fanno quattro.*"

Sarah suddenly got a chill. All her years as a bureaucrat chained to a desk, was she now really in such danger? "Well, nothing will happen while I'm here. I'll eat lunch in the office."

Alberto agreed but added, "But the risky time is when you go home. I suggest you take steps to reduce the risk."

"Thanks, Alberto. I'll do that. Any luck on decrypting the file?"

"Not yet. I think I am making progress but it is a difficult task."

"OK, Alberto. Thank you." She put the anonymous phone back in her bag and reached for her pistol. She checked that it was loaded and put it back. She called Bill Armitage. "Bill, I want to give you an update. It appears as if the deal was transacted and the phony file was discovered. My techie who substituted the file, warned me that if they think I know where the real file is, I am in trouble."

"He's probably right. I should get you an escort to take you home tonight?"

"I don't think that's necessary. Even if you do, then what? Someone going to stay with me all night?"

"If necessary. Why not?" he added.

"No. don't be silly. I'll be careful." Then she let out a painful chuckle and added, "But if I don't show up tomorrow morning, send a posse after me."

"That's not funny. At the very least, call me when you get into your apartment."

"I'll do that." As soon as she hung up, she called Tony and repeated what she had just told Armitage.

"My God, Alberto's right. They will stop at nothing to get the file. If they grab you, they will squeeze Alberto's identity out of you before they kill you."

"I'll be OK. Don't worry."

"Sarah, you are making much too light of this. These people have already killed and are probably now desperate."

"What should I do? Armitage offered me an escort but that's not enough if what you say is true."

Tony thought for a minute. "Disappear," he said.

"What? Disappear? How?" she said.

"Leave your office now. Tell your assistant, Armand - isn't that his name? - that you'll be back in an hour. Dentist or something like that. Don't let on that you're not coming back."

"Then what?"

"Get in your car. Don't go home. Drive up to New York and meet me."

"How can I do that? No clothes, No nothing."

"Do it. These people are not playing around. And they will definitely be in a hurry. Come right to my office. Park outside. I'll see that you don't get a parking ticket. If you leave now, you should be here by eight or nine."

"I have an ugly thought. If they are that anxious, do you think they might be waiting for me at my car in the garage, like before."

"That's very possible," he said. "In fact, the more I think about it, you shouldn't take a chance."

"If you think it's that serious, I'll can take a cab to the station and take the next train." She looked at her watch. "I can make the 5:10. It'll get me into Penn Station about 9:30. Meanwhile, if they wanted to intercept me in the garage, they will be waiting. Can you meet me at Penn Station so late?"

He laughed. "Of course. Do it now and call me from the train so I know you're on it."

"See you later." She opened the office door. Armand looked up. "I'm going up to twelve to see the boss. I'll be back in about twenty minutes or so. Take messages."

"You got it," he answered with a smile.

Instead of going up, she took the elevator down paying attention to her surroundings. Alberto and Tony had made her very wary. She was now really scared. As she walked outside, paying attention to her surroundings, she saw no one and hailed a cab. "Union Station." she said, and hurry please."

"I think we're OK, traffic-wise, Ma'am. We beat the rush hour."

"Hope so." The ride to the station was very fast. She bought a ticket, checked the departure board for the track number and went right to the platform. It was 4:50. So far, so good, she thought. The train came in at 5:00 and she boarded with the crowd of waiting passengers. She waited apprehensively until the train pulled out. She called Tony. "I'm on my way. Nothing unusual so far."

"That's good. The train gets in at 9:25. I checked. I'll meet you then."

"Thanks, Tony. See you later." She called her office and got her voice mail. Armand had evidently already left. Just then, her regular cell phone rang. A blocked number. She denied the call and turned the phone off completely. She remembered her techie telling her to turn off her computer. She thought that turning off her phone would provide the same kind of security. You can't hack a phone when it's off, she thought. With the right software, they could access her GPS. She hoped they hadn't done so already. The rest of the ride was uneventful but she was too strung out to leave her seat. She called Tony when she was a half hour out of Penn Station. "Looks like I'm on time. I did get a phone call about 5:30 from a blocked number."

"Did you answer?"

"No, and I turned off the phone. I'll use this one for the time being."

"You hungry?"

"Absolutely starved. I skipped lunch. I haven't had anything since my cinnamon bun at Panera this morning."

Tony was waiting for her when she got off the train and smiled broadly when he saw her. She said nothing, just walked up and hugged him. "Let's eat," he said and took her arm. "Trip OK?"

"It was fine except it was hours of confused thinking and riding in fear. I have not the foggiest idea who's involved in this. The only one that seems to be giving off vibes is Henry Stafford. Bill Armitage has been looking into him and there have been some hints he's involved. But nothing sure yet."

"I would think that they'll have to show themselves a little more because they haven't got the file to sell. They have to find it so they can't hide completely especially since people are looking now. Before, no one was paying attention."

"You're probably right. But what am I going to do? I can't stay in New York for any length of time."

They went into a small cafe on 34th street and sat down. A waiter came up to them and asked if they wanted something to drink. Tony looked up at Sarah. "Nothing for me," she said. "I'll have something with my meal."

After they ordered, Tony said, "Here's what I suggest. I assume that things are going to happen very fast now that the deal apparently failed. I would also assume there's a lot of money at stake. That usually pushes things. Why don't you stay in New York for, say, two days and wait it out a little. Is there anyone you can trust at the office?"

"The only one, I think, and I'm not absolutely sure is Bill Armitage. He's the security chief. He's the one looking into Stafford and then there's my assistant. My instincts are that he's straight as an arrow but I wouldn't risk trusting him."

"How about your boss?" he asked.

"I would trust him about this thing but he's so slow-witted, I would be afraid to trust him with any information. He'd screw things up."

"OK, then call Armitage and tell him what's going on. Ask him to call your boss and tell him you will be gone a couple of days. Then he should call Armand and tell him the same thing."

"Should I update Armand on what's happening?" she asked.

"You said you weren't sure about him."

"I don't know. Every indication is that he's worried about me, but I just don't know."

"Then he's probably OK, but just the same, I'd restrict information to Armitage. The fewer who know, the better."

She looked at her watch. "I'll call him in the morning."

When they finished eating, Tony paid the bill even though Sarah reached for it unsuccessfully. "What do you want to do about tonight?" he asked. "You can get a hotel room or you can crash at my apartment. I promise to behave."

She laughed, "That's the last thing I'm worried about. Frankly, I'd love to stay at a hotel but I'm just not happy being alone, tonight. I'm not used to this kind of stress. I'm a desk jockey."

"OK. My apartment it is."

"Is there a pharmacy open nearby? Toothbrush and stuff."

"Sure, there's a Duane Reade nearby. Let's go."

At the pharmacy, Sarah got what she needed and even found some underwear to hold her until she could get to a store in the morning. Tony's apartment was on 72nd street and as soon as they entered the building, Sarah felt somewhat relieved. When they entered the apartment, she looked around and put her shopping bag on the table. "Nice place, for a guy," she said.

He laughed. "I'm Italian. We have class. You take the bed," he said. "I can sleep on the couch. It's a sleeper."

"You sure?" she asked, not wanting to inconvenience him.

He shook his head. "TV remote on the night table Let me use the bathroom first, then it's yours for the night."

After Sarah said goodnight, Tony called Alberto and updated him on what was happening on their end. "I have decrypted the file." Alberto replied.

"Wow. What did you find?"

"Five of the most powerful NSA hacking tools I have ever seen. They would be worth a fortune for intelligence purposes. I see why they must be very upset. I would love to know how much they are being sold for."

"So would I. But for now, be careful, Alberto. If they are frantically looking for the file, they may well stumble onto you and find out where you are. I don't know how effective they are but you have to assume that with NSA connections, they may have the necessary knowhow and resources to find you."

"I agree. I'll be careful."

CHAPTER XI

May 19th - telephone activity

Herman listened. "I agree. We must find her. There can't be anyone else. I will ask Henry to try to find out where she is."

"The fact that we can't find her reinforces my idea that she knows what is happening," was the answer. "The other thing you can do is push Theodore to get to the Italian intruder. It just may not be an accident that whoever it is can block himself."

"I will push him but up to now he has not been able to do it. He has tried."

"Threaten him to light a fire under him."

"I will. Is there anything else?" Herman asked.

"No, just do what you have to, but find her and quickly."

Herman called Stafford. "Henry, We must find Sarah Tepper and quickly."

"Why? What's the problem?"

"The file was removed from the account and substituted. The deal is temporarily off until we can find the file. We think Sarah had something to do with it and she has conveniently disappeared. We must find her."

"It will not be easy for me. I have already inquired too much about the account and about Sarah. If I push, it will expose me. The risk is very great."

"See what you can do, but don't jeopardize yourself."

"I'll try. I'll call you later."

Stafford went to Sarah's office. Armand asked him, "May I help you Mr. Stafford?"

"Sarah in?" he asked.

"No, she called that she will be away for a couple of days."

"Vacation?"

"I don't think so. Just away."

"Oh. Where?"

"I don't know, Mr. Stafford. She didn't say. Why are you so interested?" Armand asked.

"Just curious. When will she be back?"

"The only word I got was a couple of days. I tried to call her cell phone but she doesn't answer it."

"Maybe Manson knows. I'll go up and see him. Thanks, Armand."

"Sorry, I couldn't help."

Stafford took the elevator to the twelfth floor and asked Manson's secretary if he was in. "Yes, but he's on the phone, Mr. Stafford. Let me drop a note on his desk and let him know you are here."

"Thanks."

She wrote on a post-it and walked into Manson's office. When she came back, she said, "He said he'll be off the phone in a minute. Why don't you have a seat?"

"Thanks." He sat down. A minute later, Manson opened his door and waved Stafford in."

"How are you Henry? What can I do for you?"

"I'm great, Stuart. I was looking for Sarah. They said she was away for a couple of days. I wanted to ask her a favor. Do you know where she is?"

"No, I don't, Henry. She didn't say where she was, only that she would be back in a couple of days. What kind of favor?"

"It's personal, Stu. I talked it over with her last week."

"She should be back in a couple of days. Why don't you leave a message with Armand?"

"I already did. Sorry to bother you."

"No problem. Why don't we get together for lunch one of these days. It's been a while," Manson suggested.

"Good idea, Stu. I'll call you. Take care." Stafford left and went back to his office and called Flint. "Herman. No luck. No one seems to know where she is."

"Never mind, Henry. We'll work on it." He called Theodore. "Theodore, have you found the Italian, yet?"

"No. I don't know what kind of block he is using but I can't get through it."

"I would like you to run a check on Sarah Tepper's Amex card. Can you do that?"

"I suppose I can. I have the software to hack into it."

"Then do it and call me back. I want to know the last time she used it and where." Flint paced back and forth wondering what to do next. Their megadeal was in serious danger. Is it possible someone stole the file and is trying to shortstop the sale? Then he wondered about Stafford. He was the original source of the merchandise. Would he cut his own throat? Flint couldn't make sense of it. Who knew about the file besides Sarah? He stopped pacing and poured himself a drink.

Yuri called Stafford. "Henry, I suppose you have heard by now what happened."

"Yes I have, Yuri. They are frantically searching for the stolen file. You know, if we find it first, we would be in clover if the file weren't still encrypted."

"That's no longer a problem," Yuri said.

"Why not?" Stafford asked.

"When I got the bad file, I was given the password to decrypt it. That's when we discovered the file was not the right one. If they find the file first, they will certainly change the password. But, my friend, if we find it first..." his voice trailed off.

"Let me try. It's worth a little risk for that kind of money. Call you later." Henry sat at his desk thinking. For his small share of the deal, he didn't want to take any risk of being outed. But for a huge share of the deal with Yuri, it might be worth it. But how to find the file? How? I have to find Sarah.

****

"Mr. Flint, this is Theodore."

"What have you got for me? Have you found the Italian?"

"No, still nothing on that. But I did find out that Sarah Tepper used her Amex card yesterday at H & M Department Store in New York City, the one on Fifth Avenue near Rockefeller Center. She spent $640."

"Thank you Theodore. Nice work. Keep after the Italian." Flint thought for a moment. Is she hiding? $640 clothing but why New York City? The murders, Barnhill! That must be it. He looked up the phone number of NYPD and called.

"New York Police Department. May I help you?"

"This is Herman Flint of the NSA in Washington. I would like to talk to the person in charge of the Barnhill killing several weeks ago."

"Just a moment, please."

" Detective LoPlana. Can I help you."

"This is Herman Flint at NSA in Washington. Were you involved with the Barnhill killing?"

"Yes, why?"

"I'm looking for Sarah Tepper. She said she was going up there to see someone at NYPD but I don't know who."

"We turned it over to forensics. But I think they sent everything to NSA because they had jurisdiction."

"Who is the person in forensics? Can you transfer me?"

"It was Tony Belvedere. Hold on." Herman heard the click and then ringing.

"Belvedere," was the answer.

"Mr. Belvedere. I'm Herman Flint from NSA. I'm looking for Sarah Tepper. I was told she came to see you yesterday?"

Tony wrote the name down. "No." he answered. "I haven't been in contact with her since I sent the Barnhill computer to her. Who told you she was here?"

"Stuart Manson, her division head."

"Well, she's not. We didn't have an appointment. Why don't you leave me your number. If I hear from her, I'll call you."

"That's not necessary. If she was coming to see you, you would know it already. But if she does show up, ask her to call her office. It's important and thanks."

Tony called Sarah. "Hey, Sarah. You OK?"

"Sure, Tony. Why shouldn't I be?"

"Who's Herman Flint?"

"I give up. Who's Herman Flint?"

"You don't know him?"

"Never heard of him. Who is he?"

"He just called from NSA looking for you. He said Manson told him you went to New York about the Barnhill case."

"That's bullshit. This Flint guy does not work for NSA and Stuart Manson had no clue where I am."

"Did you go shopping?"

"I needed some clothes. I had to."

"Use a credit card?"

"American Express. Uh oh. The only one who knows I'm here is Bill Armitage. If it was important, he would have called you, not some unknown flunkie. You think?"

"Yup. Someone has tools and knows something. Be careful. I'll be home in about an hour." The phone rang again. "Belvedere."

"This is Henry Stafford from NSA in Washington. Is Sarah Tepper with you?"

Tony recognized the name and Sarah's suspicion. "No, she's not, Mr. Stafford. I haven't talked to her in weeks. Is there something I can do for you?"

"No thanks, Mr. Belvedere. I'm trying to find her and I was told she came to see you."

"Why would she come to see me. Who told you that?"

"Her boss."

"Strange he would say that. Did she disappear?" he said jokingly semi-chuckling.

"No, no. She just took off for New York and didn't say why or where she was going. We just assumed it was to see you regarding the Barnhill case."

"People, especially women have been known to take off for New York on a shopping spree. Anyway, if I hear from her, I'll call you. You're at NSA? What's your extension?" Tony wrote it down. "Got it. Bye Mr. Stafford."

Tony decided not to wait. He told his colleague he was leaving and hailed a cab to take him home. He entered the building and waited in the lobby to see if anyone was following him. When he was sure there was no one, he went up to his apartment. Sarah was there watching the news on TV when he entered. "Hey, you're early." She hugged him.

"How are you?"

"Why do you keep asking me that?"

"Right after this guy Flint called, Henry Stafford called. He, too, was looking for you."

"Stafford? What on earth does he want?"

"It seems to me that there are one of two possibilities. Two guys involved in this deal are looking for the file. Or.."

"Or what?"

"There are two different deals. Two people or groups vying for the same sale."

"What do you think we should do?" she asked him. He could see the fear in her eyes.

"I'll call Alberto. It's always best to keep him up on what's happening. The more he knows the better. You call Armitage and if you still trust him, tell him who's looking for you. You said he's looking into Stafford. Tell him to see what he knows about Flint."

He called Checkov. He said LoPlana got calls from two guys looking for the Tepper woman. "She said she passed them on to you."

"Can I talk to her?"

"Sure, hang on." He passed the phone to LoPlana.

"Hey Tony, what's happening?"

"Hi. Elena. What did these guys say?"

"They both said Sarah Tepper was up here to see you. Is she?"

"No. Did they say who told them she was here?"

"As a matter of fact, they did. They both said that her boss, Stuart Manson told them. What's going on, Tony?"

"I'd rather not say, Elena. It involves the Barnhill death. I'll tell you as soon as I can. It's classified and I'm not supposed to say anything. I'm involved because I had his computer and they had to tell me something to get me to ship it to them."

"Anything you want Randy and me to do?"

"Nothing to do except if you get any more things, inquiries, whatever, regarding Sarah Tepper, let me know. And don't give up any information, none at all."

"Gotcha. Talk to you later."

"Thanks Elena, Bye." Turning to Sarah. "You still got your phone turned off?"

"Yeah, except for the anonymous one."

"Good, keep it off." He called Alberto on speaker phone. "Caro amico." He continued in English so Sarah would understand. "Sarah is with me." But before he could say more, Alberto answered.

"I know, my friend."

"How do you know?" Tony asked, a bit concerned.

"I hacked the GPS in her anonymous phone, just to see if I could find her if I had to. You never know."

Tony laughed, "Always thinking ahead. I wanted to tell you that two guys were looking for her here. No one is supposed to know she's here. They must have checked her credit card transactions. That's the only possible way they could have known she was in New York. But they didn't know why or where. They must have guessed she was visiting NYPD. They were told she wasn't here. In any case, they are looking for her. I assume these two guys are both looking for the missing file. I just don't know if they're together or separate. There could be more than one group competing for the sale."

"What are the names of the two men?" Alberto asked.

"One is Henry Stafford, who is an NSA department head. The other said he was Herman Flint, at NSA."

"Sarah had mentioned Stafford to me, once. The other name I never heard."

"She said she never heard of him either and she's sure he's not at NSA."

"That's very interesting. Stafford seems to be dirty. But I would leave him alone until we get to the bottom of everything," Alberto said. "I wouldn't want them to know we are on to them. On the other hand, we should try to find out everything we can on Flint. By the way, I was able to identify the mysterious bomber."

"Really? Who is he?" Tony asked incredulously.

"His name is Theodore Wintervale. His computer is in Virginia."

Sarah's ears perked up. "How did you manage that?"

"Ah, hello Sarah. I have my ways," he laughed. "Don't forget, I am a genius, or so my press releases say."

"We will try to find him," she replied.

"You know, I could blow him up if you wish. I can get his email address and I have his bomb generating apps." He added, "Just kidding. We may need him to get to the rest."

"I will try to find him," Sarah said.

"Anything else?" Alberto asked.

"For now, Alberto, no. Thanks for everything," Tony added a *ciao* before he hung up.

"Let mc call Armitage from your phone." She dialed.

"Armitage."

"Bill, Sarah. Two guys have been asking about me at NYPD today. The only way they would know I'm in New York is if you told them..."

He interrupted, "I hope you don't mean that."

"No. Or I wouldn't be talking to you now. I was going to add that they must've tracked my credit card, which I've used only once since I left Washington."

"Who's looking for you?" he asked.

"Henry Stafford, for one."

"That's confirming what I thought. He's in this up to his ears. Who's the other?"

"Someone named Herman Flint who said he works at NSA. I never heard of him. Did you?"

Armitage scanned the directory. "Doesn't work for NSA. I just checked."

"Can you find out who the he is?"

"I'll see what I can do. Meanwhile, watch yourself. The closer we get, the more dangerous it becomes."

"Thanks, Bill. What we don't know is if this guy Flint is working with Stafford or is a possible rival. I would think if they were working together, both of them wouldn't be looking for me."

"You're probably right. Let me see what I can find out."

"One more thing, Bill. My techie has identified the mad bomber as Theodore Wintervale, living in Virginia. See if you can find out about him too."

"Will do."

"But don't call me. My phone's off. I'll call you tomorrow," Sarah replied

"OK," he said. "Bye."

Armitage moves

Bill Armitage was too curious to wait. What Sarah said confirmed what he suspected. He did a classified search for Theodore Wintervale and it came up full. His address, email address and cell phone were all there. He was a computer expert but was currently out of work. Bill decided not to trust anyone at NSA. Instead, he called his old friend, Andrew Noble, a senior FBI agent. "Andy, Bill Armitage, I need some help from you."

"Nice, nice, Noble answered, sarcastically "I don't hear from you for months and you need my help?"

"Hey. Phone is a two way device. You got buttons too."

"OK, OK. What's up?"

Armitage explained as much as he could given the classified nature and asked Andy to find out as much as he could about this Theodore Wintervale without alerting him. He did mention the involvement of Henry Stafford at NSA and an unknown person named Herman Flint so that he would recognize the names if they popped up anywhere.

"Do you have anything that would let me show probable cause?" Andy asked. "Otherwise, I'll be breaking in without a search warrant."

"For the moment, I'm not looking for any evidence. I'm looking for information. We think he's a murderer. I just want to confirm it and find out who's paying him. So let's skip the warrant."

"Not a good idea, Bill. Besides the fact that it's not nice. If I find anything out, you can't use it in court. You know that. Get me some info on probable cause that he's dangerous and I'll get the warrant."

"OK. Can you stop and see me tomorrow, say around eleven?"

"Sure," Andy said. "You want it to be a personal friend visiting you, right?"

"You got it."

"OK, see you tomorrow, friend. Bye."

CHAPTER XII

May 20th

Andy Noble sat down in Bill Armitage's office and waited for him to get off the phone. "Hey, Bill. How're you doing?"

"Good, but let's get business out of the way before we play catch-up. Did you find out anything?" Armitage asked.

"Not a thing. The address was a room in a small warehouse absolutely empty. Someone was there, but no more."

"Was there any sign that it was occupied or you're guessing?"

Noble answered, "Only one thing. There was obviously a cable internet or TV connection but it was cut close to the wall so it was hard to see. I followed it out back to a cable box. Other than that, nothing. Someone was probably there but did a thorough clean out and clean up job."

Armitage rocked himself in his chair, a habit he picked up when he was running things through his mind. "Maybe I can find out who paid for it. But I'll do that later," he added. "Let's have lunch."

"You're not going to tell me any more?"

"Can't yet, Andy, but I appreciate what you did and I'm sure I'm going to need you again."

"Not unless you tell me something. I hate to work blind."

"I'll get clearance to tell you before I call. Let's go. I'll buy."

"That's the least you can do," he put his arm around Armitage as they walked out.

New York City

Sarah had made up her mind to stay in New York at least another day before deciding what to do and whether to return to DC. She had been shopping for several hours. In addition to the necessities she looked for, shopping took her mind off her anxiety. Without bringing anything with her, she had to get some clothes and toiletries. She tried to minimize the makeup purchases since the costs add up fast on pricey makeup items. Unfamiliar and uncomfortable with the New York subway, she hailed a cab. Getting into and out of the cab was annoying since she had several bulky bags. When she got to Tony's apartment she was suddenly wary since the door was ajar. She entered slowly and called him. "Tony." There wasn't any answer. She entered the apartment and got frightened. There had been a struggle. Broken vases were on the living room floor. She looked in the bedroom. Tony was not there. She took out her cell phone then stopped. She called Tony from his own land line. The phone went to a message. She tried again. Message again. Now she was worried. Did they get Tony? Would they come back for her? She had to hide.

She took what she needed from the bathroom, carefully closed the apartment door and hailed a cab. With her shopping bags weighing her down, the cab took her to the Beacon Hotel on Broadway. She checked in under the name of Cindy Bailey and went right to the room. She called Bill Armitage first from her anonymous cell phone and told him what she thought had happened.

"I'd be willing to bet they took him to Washington. That's where everything is happening," she said.

"You're probably right. I tapped Stafford's phones the other day. Let me check the tapes and see if I can find out anything."

"Please. This is terrible. They obviously wanted me."

"I'll get back to you. Where are you?"

"At a hotel. The less you know the better."

"OK. Can I call you on this cell phone?"

"No. I'm turning it off after I make one more call." When she hung up, she called Alberto. "Alberto, something bad has happened."

"*Cosa successo*? What, Sarah?"

"They have obviously been looking for me to get the file but somehow figured Tony was involved enough to know something so they've kidnapped him."

"*Merda*," he answered. "Let me see if I can find out something."

"How?"

"I don't know yet. But I will try."

"I'm going to get another phone and I'll call you as soon as I get it so you have the number."

"Good idea. Maybe I'll know something when you call back."

"I hope so." There was sadness in her voice.

"Don't worry, we'll find him. By the way, Theodore Wintervale has moved. I have a new address for him. I'll text it to your new phone when you call back."

Sarah left her room and asked to find the nearest cell phone store, which was right next to the hotel. She bought a new anonymous phone with minutes included. She used the name Marilyn Monroe again and paid in cash she got for shopping. When she got back to her room, she called Alberto so that he would get the new number. "I don't imagine you know anything yet," she commented as if it were a question.

"Not yet, but I am monitoring Theodore's computer to see if he makes any contact."

"Please Alberto. I'm really worried about him."

"Have a little *pazienza*, Sarah. I will continue to look. Meanwhile, call your friend Armitage and tell him everything. I'll call you as soon as I know something."

Somewhere in Virginia

Tony was sitting in a chair with a hood over his head and his hands bound behind his back. He assumed he was in the Washington DC area since the drive from his apartment was several hours. The room he was in felt like a big warehouse. It had a chilly feeling. There was no carpeting and he heard nothing. He just sat and waited. He felt to see what kind of binding was on his wrists. It was a plastic cable tie. He knew how to get out of it but he needed something with a point. But there was nothing that he could feel or think of. While he was racking his brain, he heard footsteps.

Herman Flint removed Tony's hood and spoke while the other man wearing a hood over his head with holes cut for eyes and mouth watched from behind him, saying nothing. "We are looking for Sarah Tepper. Where is she?"

"I don't know," Tony answered.

"She was with you in your apartment. Where did she go?"

"She wasn't with me," Tony said.

"You're lying. We found ladies items in your bathroom and some clothes," Flint said as the hooded man watched silently.

"You want the details of my sex life? Do I look like a monk to you?"

"She was in New York. She must have come to see you. Where is she?"

"I told you, I don't know. I told the two people who called from NSA that I didn't know because I didn't. Are you from NSA?"

"That's no concern of yours. You had better tell me where she is or it will not go well for you."

"And if I knew and were to tell you, you would let me go?"

"Well I wouldn't go that far," Flint said.

"Well then, why would I tell you anything? If the result for me will be the same."

"We will use harsher methods if need be. So make it easy on yourself."

"What difference if you kill me now or after you play your games? I told you I don't know. Ms. Tepper came to see me once after Dr. Barnhill was killed and told me very little because she told me it was classified."

The man behind him came around to the front and spoke very softly almost a whisper, as if to disguise what he really sounded like. "Mr. Belvedere. Do you know anything about the Amerada account?"

"Amerada? What the hell is that?"

"Do you know of or have you heard anything about a missing file? It's very important for us to find it and we think Ms. Tepper knows where it is. That's why we are looking for her. You can save yourself a lot of trouble and save Ms. Tepper from mistreatment if you tell us what you know."

Tony felt the back of the wooden chair he was sitting on and could feel that the wood was splintering at the end. He picked a large splintered piece from it and kept it in his hand. He repeated,

"I might tell you if I knew. But I don't know anything about what you referred to. Amerada, you said? Or a missing file. I am a forensic expert and was called in because of the strange way in which Dr. Barnhill was killed.

Flint spoke, "What do you want to do now, Mr. Galahad?"

"I do not believe him," he whispered. "Let us go. I will tell you outside what I want to do." Then looking at Tony, he said, "Mr. Belvedere. We will be back in about an hour. That should give you time to think about your future. It is up to you what happens." Then Galahad said to Flint, "Put the hood back on him. We should leave Martin outside to keep an eye on things." When they got outside, they told Martin, "Be a guard. Don't go in. We don't want anything to happen to him. You understand?" Martin nodded.

New York City

Sarah answered her phone as cryptically as possible, "Yes?"

Sarah, Alberto. They have taken him to somewhere around Washington. I tracked his cell phone but they must have taken it from him before they got to their destination. It is located at a gas station in Arlington, Virginia."

"That's a help. I have to find him. They are killers and they will kill him whether he tells them anything or not. I have to call Armitage. Thanks Alberto."

"I will keep trying to find him. Keep me posted."

"Absolutely." She called Armitage. "Bill, Tony is somewhere in this area. My techie tracked his telephone to a gas station in Arlington."

"Do you know which one?"

"No, but it was near the district."

"I'll send a couple of agents out from the FBI to see if they can track it down."

"Thanks, Bill."

"Where are you now?"

"Still in my hotel room and frantic."

"Stay there until you hear from me. Understood?"

"Yes, yes. I'm going nowhere." She took a mini-vodka and a bottle of orange juice from the refrigerator and mixed them in a glass. She guzzled it down and slumped into the arm chair.

Arlington

As soon as Flint and Galahad left, Tony worked on his bonds. It did not take long for him to push the pointed end into the locking slot, push up the locking bumps and slowly remove the band from the slot. He immediately removed his hood and looked around the warehouse. He tried the door gently, but it was locked, which did not surprise him. He listened at the door. He wondered where Martin was.

The windows were all barred. It was dark and hard to see. He looked around for and finally found the light switch. Since he was hooded, it didn't occur to them to leave a light on. He walked around the room and found a shelving section where there was scrap wood, some tools and a crow bar. He picked it up and felt its heft. At least now he had a weapon to surprise whoever was coming back. He wondered what they had done with his cell phone. They took it from him when they stopped for gas. He knew they could use it to find Sarah's anonymous number and then find her with the GPS. He wondered why they hadn't done so yet.

He continued looking around and found a shelf with paint and a gallon can of benzene. He thought for a second. He could burn the door down. It was a heavy wooden door. If it didn't burn enough to let him out, at least the fire could keep them from coming in. But the smoke might kill him if he didn't get out. There was a good chance the fire would alert the fire department, which made it worth the risk. He was sure he was destined to be disposed of like Barnhill. They certainly didn't want any witnesses.

But he needed something to start the fire. At first he couldn't find anything, then he saw it. A fifty foot extension cord. He found an electrical outlet and left the plug near the socket. Then he opened the benzene can and splashed it all over the door. He poured a large puddle under the door and then ran a wet strip of the liquid away from the door, like a fuse. He laid the half full can on top of his fuse strip and put the end of the cord into the can. He walked back to the electrical outlet and plugged the cord in. He watched while the cord short circuited just as he planned. Instead of burning, the can went off like a bomb scattering fire all over except for his fuse strip.

Where was Martin? He must have heard the explosion. He ripped a piece of his sleeve off , wet it with benzene to make a torch and lit it from one of the scattered blazes. He lit his benzene fuse which went up in flames and then the started the door burning. He backed off and waited. After a few minutes, he screamed, "Help, help." Then he heard someone trying to get the door open. He went to the burning door and waited next to it with the crow bar. Someone kicked the door which crashed off its hinges. Martin stepped in holding a pistol. Tony slammed the crowbar down on the gun hand making Martin drop it. Then he swing the crowbar like a baseball bat at Martin, hitting him in the throat. He dropped like a stone. Tony didn't wait to see if he was still alive.

He took the crow bar with him and ran outside. No one else was babysitting him so he watched from behind a fence while the whole building burst into flames. He walked through the parking lot to the road and waited for a car or truck to come. He had no idea where he was. He only assumed he was in the Washington area. Finally after about ten minutes, a truck passed by and stopped for him.

"Where you going?" the driver asked.

"Next town," Tony answered.

"Get in. Next town is Washington. You OK?"

"Where am I?" he asked.

"You really don't know?" he answered. "You're in Arlington."

"You going into DC?"

"Sure am. Wow, look at that fire," he said as the building exploded."

"I would appreciate the ride."

"You want to tell me what's with you?" he said as he gunned the engine.

"My name's Tony Belvedere. The only thing I can say is that I'm with the New York City police department and I was kidnapped and brought here. I escaped, and the rest is classified and I appreciate the lift. The only other thing I can say is that you probably saved my life. My kidnappers were supposed to come back for a torture session and then..." he ran his finger across his throat.

"Well fuck me. What a story. My name's Bob Styczynski but most people call me Stash for obvious reasons." He reached his hand out and Tony shook it. "You wanna call anyone? I got a cell phone."

"Great. Yes." He looked at his watch. He dialed Alberto. "*Ciao, Alberto.*"

"Tony. Sei vivo?"

"*Si, si. Son stato rapito. Ho riuscito scappare, e poi bruciato l'edificio. Penso che sia una specie di magazzino, vuoto.*"

He told Alberto how he escaped and burned down the warehouse, then asked if he talked to Sarah. Alberto told Tony she was worried and gave Tony her new phone number. "*Sai tuo telefono si trova a Arlington. Dove sei?*"

"Arlington. *Grazie amico. Ciao, ci parliamo domani.*" Looking at Stash, he asked, "Do you mind if I make another call?"

"Nah, be my guest."

He called Sarah. "Hey, it's me."

"Tony? Where are you?"

"Arlington, just escaped. I was taken by some guys. They grabbed me, put a hood over my head and drove me to Arlington. They wanted you or the file."

"Where are you now?"

"In a truck. A nice guy stopped for me after I got out and burned the place down. I'm on my way to DC."

"Why don't you go to my apartment." She told him the address where there was a key taped to the back of a large flowerpot in the hall. "Call me from there. But be careful."

"Where are you?" he asked.

"In a hotel. Better you don't know which."

He laughed. "Don't worry. Talk to you later. I don't want to abuse this driver's phone." He handed the driver his phone. "Thanks."

"Where do want to go?"

"I don't know DC very well." He told the driver the address.

"I can't go there with this truck. But I can drop you a few blocks away. Is that OK?"

"That's great. I really appreciate it."

Just then, breaking news came on the truck radio. It announced an old empty warehouse in Arlington was burned to the ground. An unidentified man was found inside burned beyond recognition. The fire department suspects arson. The driver looked at Tony. "You do that?"

"Couldn't really help it. It was the only way I would get away without getting shot. But that's another story. Suffice to say, I got away. I was a dead man if I had stayed."

"Wow." He looked and pointed. "If I let you off here, you go down there about four blocks. That's the street."

"Thanks, Stash. Leave me your phone number. I'll tell you how it all ends. You deserve at least that."

Stash pulled a company card out of the glove compartment and wrote his phone number. "Here. I'm curious to know. Take care."

Tony got out of the truck and walked to Sarah's apartment building. It was dark but he saw two men waiting outside under a street lamp. He walked right past them. They were obviously waiting for someone they would recognize. It obviously wasn't him, but it was probably Sarah.

Armitage

FBI Agent Gary Schwinn called Bill Armitage. "Mr. Armitage. This is agent Schwinn. We couldn't find the gas station but this warehouse in the area that was burned down, they found a guy burned to a crisp in it. It was arson. I don't know if it's the guy we're looking for."

"I sure as shit hope not. It might be where he was being held. Unless you think there's someplace else to look, give it up for the day. I'll let Andy know." He dialed Sarah. "I've got some possible bad news, Sarah."

"What? Tell me."

"A warehouse was burned down in Arlington and they found an unidentified dead guy inside burned to a crisp. We don't know if it was Tony."

"No, no. Tony's OK," she answered. "He called me a little while ago. He managed to escape and needed fire to get past the guy watching him. The result was he burned the place down when he escaped. The guy there was his armed baby sitter."

"That's good news. I was worried."

"I told Tony to go to my apartment. He's probably there now. Why don't you call my land line. He might just pick it up. Meanwhile, I'm coming back to Washington on the train. I'll call you from the station when I get to DC. For an escort," she added.

"Planning to go home?"

"You betcha. I can't live like this. We've got to get to the bottom of this thing soon so I can get back to being a desk jockey. I never thought I would say that."

"Maybe we should get you trained as an operative."

"Not on your life. I am definitely not cut out for this," she answered. "I'm getting a call from my apartment. I'll call you later. Hello."

"Sarah, I'm here. There are two guys outside probably waiting for you. They ignored me."

"I'm coming back to DC. My plan is to call Bill when I get to the DC station for an escort to my apartment. Bill is going to call you on my line."

"That's good. Meanwhile, I'm starved. Do you mind if I scramble myself some eggs?"

She laughed. "I'm a cheap date. You eat my food."

"I'll make it up to you, Promise."

"Hopefully, I'll see you later."

Several minutes later, Tony answered a call from Armitage. "Tony, this is Bill Armitage. You OK?"

"Sure. There are two guys downstairs waiting for someone, Sarah I would guess."

"I'll come with a couple of FBI agents when she gets here. We can pick them up then."

"Maybe you should wait until they try to grab her."

"No. I'm not going to use Sarah as bait. If they're involved, we'll get it out of them. Don't worry."

"You're right. Sorry I suggested it. I just wanted to make sure you could charge them with something. It's hard to charge stalkers who don't do anything. Meanwhile, I'll catch a nap. It's been a tough night and I'm exhausted. Then I'll meet Sarah at the station and call you."

DC

Sarah called her office and left a message for Armand that she was coming back and would be in the office in the morning. She went downstairs, found a luggage store nearby and got a small suitcase for all the stuff she bought. She didn't like traveling with shopping bags. She packed her clothes and checked her pistol to make sure it was loaded and then gave one last look in the mirror and went down to check out. She hailed a cab to take her to Penn Station. Since this affair started, she became more in touch with her surroundings. But she resisted the paranoia that tends to creep in when one is frightened. She had made up her mind she was not going to let this Amerada thing ruin her life.

Tony checked his watch and went to meet Sarah at the train station. Armitage with the FBI agents would be going directly to Sarah's apartment. But when Armitage got to Sarah's, there was no one apparently waiting for her. They looked all over and saw no one. Armitage called Tony.

"Tony, there was no one at Sarah's apartment. Do you think they plan to meet her at the station?"

"How would they know that she was coming and that she would take the train, not the plane?"

"I have no clue," Armitage answered. "She does prefer the train. I think they could guess that. But that she was coming tonight, I don't know. In any case, keep your eyes open at the station. Would you recognize them if you saw them?"

"I think so," Tony answered. "They might recognize me since they saw me at Sarah's. I'll keep out of sight but with eyes open."

"We'll wait here at Sarah's until you get here. Call me when she get's in, OK?"

"Will do. Bye." He hung up and looked around. There was no sign of the two men. But when he went to the platform and as the train pulled in, he saw them keeping in plain sight in a crowd of people waiting to board the train. He called Armitage. "They're here Bill. I'm concerned."

"On our way."

Tony watched and saw Sarah exiting from the train. The two men came out of the crowd toward her. Tony reached Sarah first and before she could say anything, he turned her around and forced her back onto the train with the people boarding. They sat down in a seat with a window facing the platform. "What the fuck, Tony?"

"Sarah, glad to see you. Look." He pointed to the two men that were waiting for her to get off. "Armitage is on his way here with FBI agents."

"Hey, I know those two guys. They're the ones that attacked me in the garage, the ones Armand saved me from," she said excitedly, took her gun out of her purse and cocked it.

"When'd you get that?"

"Had it a long time. Never had any desire to use it. I just took it out of mothballs and spent a couple of hours at the gun range to refresh myself."

He looked at her with a frown. "That worried, huh? OK. Let's get off the train now and keep together staying in a crowd. Walk fast with me. They will probably follow us looking for a proper time to grab you. If they come after us, I don't mean follow us, I mean get close to us, turn, stop and point the gun at one of them so they can see it."

"What will you do?"

"I will jump them. Just do what I said. Don't run away. Just point the gun. If they eliminate me as a threat, then shoot. Don't hesitate. Shoot."

"OK, OK" she said, reluctantly. They walked fast toward the information booth and when Tony saw a cop, he led Sarah toward him.

"Officer Manino," Tony read his name tag and then flashed his badge. "I'm Tony Belvedere from NYPD forensics and this is Sarah Tepper from NSA. I'm unarmed but Ms. Tepper has a pistol. We are being followed by two men who are after Ms. Tepper."

"I think I see them," he nodded. "One is a blond?"

"That's them."

"Put your gun away, Ma'am." He pulled his gun out of the holster. "They've walked away and are standing against the ticket machine."

Tony answered, "Probably waiting for us to leave. If you don't mind, continue talking to us. Someone is coming to meet us with FBI agents. Ms. Tepper is in danger. They want information from her."

"What kind of information?" he asked.

Sarah interjected, "Sorry officer, it's classified and I can't tell you."

They continued their conversation and the two men continued to wait. Several minutes later, Tony's phone rang. "Where are you, Tony?" Armitage asked.

"Right at the info booth with a policeman."

"Ah. I see you." As soon as Armitage with two agents arrived, the two men disappeared. "Where are they?" Armitage asked.

Tony answered, "Gone. As soon as they saw you coming."

Armitage introduced himself and the FBI agents to Officer Manino. Tony thanked him before they all left and got into Armitage's car.

Galahad

"I'm sorry, Mr. Galahad. There was nothing we could do. They were with a policeman and then three others arrived."

Galahad replied very quietly, "Time is getting critical, Michael. I want the two of you to wait at her apartment until there are no agents watching and then go in and get her. I don't care how."

"What if that man is with her? The one who met her at the station."

"That may be the man that burned down our warehouse and killed Martin. Kill him if you have to. I want her now," Galahad replied. "Do you understand?"

"Where should we bring her when we get her."

"Call me from your car when you have her and I will tell you. Make sure you have a hood over her head."

"OK, we'll go now." Michael looked at the other man and said. "He wants us to grab her now as soon as the agents leave her apartment."

"And the guy she was with?"

Michael said nothing. He just looked at the other man who understood.

Sarah's apartment

"Can I get you all something? A drink? Something?" Sarah offered when they got to her apartment.

"No, thanks, we're fine," Armitage said after looking at the others. "Do you want us to position an agent outside in case they try something?"

"I think we'll be Ok, Bill," Tony said. "We won't answer the door. Sarah wants to go to her office tomorrow. I'll stay with her and escort her to her office in the morning."

"Do you want a gun?"

Tony was surprised at the question. "That would make me feel better if you could arrange it."

"I'll send one over by messenger in a big box. He will knock three times twice. Don't answer for anyone else,"

"Sounds mysterious," Tony answered, with a smile.

"These guys are not playing, Tony. Be careful. They obviously need her to get the files they want so badly? Do you have it?" he asked.

"No, but they're on the server. And they suspect that I either have them or know where to find them. I'm the only one that could know, the only one that has an interest in it."

Tony answered, "Remember, Sarah, there were two people looking for you in New York and we had the idea that they might not be together. There may be two entities coming after you."

"Tony, I'll leave two agents outside until the messenger comes back with the gun. They'll leave then. Call me in the morning. I'll send an escort for both of you. If anything happens tonight, call my cell phone."

"Thanks, Bill. You've been great."

An hour later, the messenger came as agreed with a Glock automatic and three clips of ammunition. Tony loaded one in but did not cock it. "Sarah, I have an idea. We're not looking for trouble. Is there a basement exit in this building?"

"Yes, there is. Why?"

"Why don't we leave?"

"And do what?"

"Doesn't matter. Your car is still in the garage at the office, right?"

"Yeah, it is."

"Then let's do this. I know it's late but let's get a cab, get your car and go for a drive. Kill a few hours. Then we can come back and see if anything happened at your apartment."

"Sounds like fun. I slept for a couple of hours on the train so I'm wide awake. How about you?" she asked.

"I napped a bit before. I'm OK. Let's do it now, before the agents leave."

They left the apartment, locked the door and took the elevator down to the basement. Tony took out the Glock, cocked it and looked at Sarah. "Just in case it stops at the lobby and there are visitors." The elevator continued and went right to the basement. They got out and Sarah led the way through the garage, laundry room and storage section to the side entrance. "Wait here," Tony went out to the street cautiously and hailed a cab. When it stopped, he waved to Sarah who came running out. They got into the cab, and told the driver where to go. As they passed the front of the building, they did not see anyone waiting. The agents were gone and the two men were not there. They relaxed and Sarah put her head on Tony's shoulder and grabbed his arm.

"This is the first minute I've been relaxed in several days."

He laughed. "I'm just lucky to be alive. There is no doubt in my mind that they were going to try to torture your location out of me and then, no witnesses."

"I wonder what they thought when they returned to find the place up in flames."

"I just wish I could recognize the man that was wearing a hood. I strain my mind to think if there was anything distinct about him, something I would recognize if I ever saw him again. The other guy, I would definitely recognize. I guess he didn't expect me to be around to identify him," Tony speculated. "I would imagine I'm in his sights, now."

The cab let them off at the garage exit of Sarah's NSA building. They walked down the ramp to the first level. The garage was almost empty except for Sarah's car and two others. Tony was cautious and looked around to be sure they were alone. They got to the car and Sarah got into the driver's side. "You want to drive?" Tony asked her.

"Sure. I need the action. You OK with that?"

"Oh, yeah," he said. "Let's go."

"Where to?"

"Where can we get something to eat? I'm suddenly ravenous," he asked.

"I know," she said. They drove to Maryland, through Silver Spring and found a strip mall on Georgia Avenue with an all night diner. Their meal was quiet. Obviously, both of them had a hectic day and were just relaxing. Neither of them felt much like talking. The crowning point of the meal was a glass of wine for each of them.

Tony looked at his watch. "Let's go back and see what's going on."

"You sure you want to do that?" she asked. "Not too much time has passed since we left."

"Unless you want to get a hotel room," he asked, looking for her expression.

"Tony, I would love to make love to you, and your suggestion is tempting but let's wait for a better day. OK?"

He smiled and kissed her on the forehead. Let's go back and face the music."

Galahad

"I don't understand. They aren't there? Where are they?"

"I don't know, Mr. Galahad. I saw them go into the building and didn't see them leave. We broke into their apartment. They weren't there."

"Michael, this is beginning to annoy me. There is a great deal at stake. You are forcing me to find someone competent to do a simple thing."

"We'll find her, Mr. Galahad. I promise. We will wait in her apartment. They must come back. She has to get dressed to go to her office in the morning."

"That's not a sure thing, Michael. But for the moment, do that. Wait in the apartment. And if they come back, please don't give me any more excuses. Bring her with a hood over her head to Theodore's residence. He's not there any more. If they don't show up by morning, call me."

"What about him?" Michael asked.

"If he is in the way, remove him as I've told you. Permanently, if necessary."

Michael and Eric went back up to Sarah's apartment and waited quietly. Michael took the hood out of his pocket and cocked his automatic. Eric cocked his and they both sat comfortably on the couch and waited in the dark.

Sarah and Tony

Sarah drove past the front of the building. "So far, so good," Tony said. "There doesn't seem to be any sign of them." Sarah drove around to the garage entrance. "Go very slowly down the ramp, Sarah." He cocked his Glock. When they got into the garage, Tony said, "Drive around the garage slowly before you park in your space." She said nothing and did as he asked. Tony looked carefully but there was no sign of anyone and no place to hide except behind a car and Tony saw nothing.

"Should I park now?"

"Yeah. Just do everything slowly."

They got out of the car. Tony kept his gun in hand and they walked to the elevator. Sarah hit number 5, and the elevator door closed. They said nothing. When the elevator reached 5, they got out and walked quietly to her apartment. Tony's forensic instinct saw immediately that the door lock was broken. He took Sarah away from the door and whispered to her. "You go in. They won't hurt you. They need your information. Just do whatever they want. They will try to take you. Don't fight, just go."

"I'm scared, Tony."

"Don't be. Just do what I said and trust me. If they ask where I am, say you dropped me at the Woodner hotel."

Sarah put her key in the door as if she was unaware it was broken and opened the door. When she turned on the light, she saw two men holding a gun on her. "Sit down, Ms. Tepper."

"Who are you? What do you want?" she said in a stunned tone.

"Come, come. You know. Where is your boyfriend?" She didn't answer. "Your boyfriend," he raised his voice.

"I dropped him at a hotel."

"Which one?" She didn't answer. "Which one?" he repeated louder.

"The Woodner."

"Put your hands behind your back, please." Sarah did what he asked. Eric bound her with plastic cable ties. Martin put a hood over her head. "Let's go." He took her arm and pulled her toward the door. When they got past the door jamb, Tony crushed his Glock over Michael's head and he collapsed. A split second later, he shot Eric between the eyes.

"You OK, Sarah?"

"Now I am. I was scared shitless. How did you know to do that?"

"I got my citizenship by serving in the marines. I was well trained. Give me your phone." He called Armitage and told him what happened. In ten minutes, three policemen from the DC police were there. Within the hour, they were all gone and everything was cleaned up. They went into the apartment.

"I gotta get an hour or two of sleep," Sarah said.

"I'll nap on the couch. Go do your thing." He kissed her on the lips gently and she hugged him. "Go, get some sleep."

"The door lock is broken," she said. "Is that OK?"

He smiled. "I don't expect we'll be bothered any more tonight. We can get it fixed tomorrow. Besides, I'm here to protect you," he said with a huge grin. "Go."

CHAPTER XIII

May 21st

Sarah was surprised when she walked into the office with Tony. Armand seemed genuinely glad to see her. "Great to see you Sarah. I was really worried about you."

"I'm fine. I'm fine. Anything happen of consequence while I was gone?"

"Not really. Where were you?" he asked. "You just disappeared so suddenly. You gotta admit it was a little puzzling."

"New York City visiting a friend. I've been threatened so I decided to leave suddenly. You've met Tony before, but let me formally introduce you. This os Tony Belvedere from NYPD forensics, investigating the Barnhill case."

"Nice to meet you, Armand," Tony said.

"Same here," Armand answered. "Have you found out anything about that Barnhill killing?"

"Not much. We just have an idea how it was done. Other than that, nothing."

"No idea who did it or why?" Armand asked. Tony shook his head.

"Come on in," Sarah said to Tony, opening the door to her office for him. He went in and sat down. She went behind her desk and looked over it before she sat down. "I know he saved me but, I don't know why, I just don't feel comfortable with him."

"I can understand it. He's not the warmest person I've ever met. His concern doesn't feel genuine to me."

"It's not as if I had any particular closeness with him before this incident. It was always arms length and he, I think, preferred it that way himself."

"So what's the problem?" Tony asked.

"It's just that lately, he seems more friendly. It's out of character. He's been cold and businesslike for years. Suddenly, he takes an interest in me, my safety." She shook her head. "Maybe I'm just being paranoid."

"I can understand your discomfort, given what's happened lately." he said. "You're right to be watchful and careful but you're not being paranoid. They really are out to get you, as Woody Allen once said. Do me a favor before I go. Call my regular phone."

Sarah called from her office line and handed the phone to Tony when it started ringing. A feminine voice answered, "Hello."

"Miss, you are talking on my phone. May I ask where you found it and where you are now?" he asked.

It was a young voice that responded. "I found it on the floor in the lobby of a building on 72nd Street. I tried to call the owner but it was passworded."

"Where are you now?"

"I don't want to tell you, that," she said apprehensively. "I don't know you."

"I can appreciate that. How can I get the phone back?"

"What's your name?" she asked.

"Tony Belvedere. What's yours?"

"Eleanor. How about this? I'll leave the phone in an envelope with your name on it. You know the newsstand on the corner?"

"Yes, and he knows me."

"I'll leave it with him, OK?"

"That's fine. And I really appreciate the trouble. If you see your way clear when you talk to the newsstand guy to tell me how to reach you, I would like to reward you for your trouble. In fact, I'll leave something in that envelope for you."

"OK, but that won't be necessary. I'll leave it with him this afternoon."

"Thank you, Eleanor," he hung up. Looking at Sarah, he said, "I dropped that phone on purpose in the lobby. I didn't want them to get it. My anonymous phone must still be in the apartment. We're lucky though, Alberto's phone number is on that phone. By the time they decided to look for it on my person, I had already dropped it. Where can I get a phone?"

"Radio Shack downstairs." She called the anonymous phone. It rang and then went to message. "Message," She said looking at him.

"Great. How about I come back about 12:30 for lunch?"

"Please. I'm scared to death to be alone."

"And I'm scared to leave you alone when you leave here. At least until this thing is settled. See you later." Tony left and when he said goodbye to Armand added. "Armand. keep an eye on Sarah."

"Is she in some kind of trouble?" Armand asked.

"Sort of. Nothing serious but she's worried so watch out for her."

Will do," he answered with a smile. "Take care."

Galahad

"What's the story, Mr. Galahad? Do you have the merchandise?"

"Not yet, Yuri. We have had some problems. But, not to worry. They will be straightened out soon."

"I hope so. We have been counting on this. My superiors are slow moving, as you know. But when they finally settle on something, they become impatient."

Galahad knew that Yuri's people could not get this from anyone else and they had no leverage. They would just have to wait. The deal would not expire. "We are as anxious as you are to consummate this deal. So until we resolve this problem, you will just have to wait. I will contact you when things are resolved."

"I hope it's soon, Mr. Galahad. Goodbye." Yuri called Henry Stafford. "Where do we stand, Henry? What's going on?"

"I don't know. Last I checked, the Amerada file was there."

"But that was the fake one, Henry. Can you find out what the story is?"

"It's very difficult, Yuri, if not impossible. I'm trying to keep a low profile. Up to now, I've been asking questions but if I keep it up, the red flags will go up. In fact, I hope I haven't already done too much. That's why I'm trying to back off."

"Something has gone amiss with this deal and I don't know what it is."

"I will see what I can find out but I have to be careful."

"I understand. Let me know as soon as you find anything."

"I will do that, Yuri. Meanwhile, be patient. They want the deal as much as we do."

Tony in DC

Tony sat on a bench in the small park across from Sarah's office and set up his new phone. As soon as he finished, he called

Alberto. "Ciao, Alberto. This is my new cell phone. You now have the number. Anything new on your end?"

"Nothing, really. I have been trying to hack into the computer of the Russian whose activity stopped suddenly. I've had no luck. It is possible that it was put out of commission. There hasn't been any activity at all since it stopped."

"Do you think it was bombed?"

"It is certainly a possibility. If they were as sensitive as their past behavior indicated, it could be."

"Do something for me, if you can. Find out where my anonymous phone is. I need to know if it's still where I left it in my apartment. Your phone number is on it. I wouldn't want them to find you."

"That's not difficult. I'll let you know."

"I'm having lunch with Sarah but I have to return to New York later. I'm going to call Armitage and arrange for her to have proper protection. She is their only real possibility to find out where the file is. I'm really concerned. You might monitor the location of her phone to make sure you can keep tabs on her."

"I'll do that. I'll call you later," Alberto said.

A little past noon, Tony went back to Sarah's building. Armand wasn't there and Tony walked into her office. She was poring over her computer when she looked up at Tony and smiled. "Is it that time already?" she said.

"Sure is. Where's Armand?"

"Out to lunch. Let's go. I'm starving." She got up and put her coat on. Tony could see that she was afraid. He didn't want to leave but he had to see what was going on in his apartment. He worried that they found something that would give them information. She didn't have much to say but was holding on to his arm very tightly. When they got to the elevator, she still wouldn't let go.

"You OK, Sarah? You're holding my arm like you've got white knuckles."

"Sorry. I'm scared like I've never been."

"What are you afraid of?"

"That's the problem. I don't know. I just have this feeling that I'm sitting on the edge of Mount Doom and I'm going to fall in with Frodo's ring."

He laughed. "I have to go back to New York this afternoon. I called Alberto who will keep track of where you are. I called Armitage and he will give you proper protection. He'll see that you get escorted home and will post a guard at your apartment."

"Do you really have to go?" she asked with a slight whine in her voice.

"Yes. I have to tell my boss what's happened and I want to see the situation at my apartment."

"I locked it when I left after they kidnapped you."

"That's good but breaking into it wouldn't be so hard. I want to be sure I left nothing that would give them any kind of lead."

"When will you come back?"

"Tell you what. I'll fly up, catch the first flight when I leave you back in your office and try to fly back later tonight. Will that make you feel any better?"

"Much. I have this feeling that there are people looking for me but I don't know who and from what direction they're coming."

"That's very perceptive, my sweet. And I don't want to upset you but it's probably true. Until we find out who's behind this, you're going to have to live with it. But there are people involved who are doing what is necessary to protect you, including me, so the risk is minimal."

They walked to a small cafe two blocks away, Sarah still clinging to him for dear life. Lunch was quiet and Sarah relaxed somewhat. She did refuse a glass of wine. "Sure you don't want any?"

"On one hand, it would relax me. On the other, I don't want to dull any of my senses or reflexes."

"Very practical," he said. "You want to be the designated victim?"

"Very funny. I am the designated victim. Unfortunately I was elected and did not choose to run."

"Is this a great country or what?" he stifled a laugh.

"That's not funny." she dipped a piece of bread in olive oil.

"Sorry. I don't mean to make light of things. But a little laughter doesn't mean we've let our guards down. In fact, if you look through the window at the building across the street, there are two men that have been waiting there for at least ten minutes. Do you recognize them?"

Sarah looked. "Of course. They're the same two guys that assaulted me and waited for us in the station."

"That's what I thought." He took out his phone and called Bill Armitage. "Bill, Tony Belvedere." He paused. "Having lunch with Sarah. I want to give you a heads up. Those two guys that disappeared in the station. They're waiting across the street from Adolph's Cafe on Connecticut. I think you should have the FBI pick them up while we wait in the cafe. We'll sit here until you do. Thanks."

They finished their lunch and as they were having their coffee, Tony pointed to the window. Three men were escorting the two men away. "I don't know if the FBI has grounds to hold them. They may ask you to identify them as the ones who assaulted you in the garage. Let's go. The sooner I can get to New York, the sooner I can come back."

Sarah took out her credit card and Tony stopped her. "Hey, this is a business lunch. Uncle Sam will pay it," she said. "Don't fight me on this."

"OK, OK. Thanks for lunch."

"Never mind. Thanks for being here. I just feel so dependent on people. I'm not an investigator. I'm waiting for someone to figure out what this is all about. Meanwhile, I know I'm a target and there's nothing I can do about it."

"Not true. Things are being done about it. You need a little patience." When they got to Sarah's office, Armand was sitting at his computer.

"Ah. There you are," Armand said. "Bill Armitage called."

"Any message?"

"Just to call him. I asked what it was about. He said it wasn't important. He just had a question to ask you."

"Thanks. You leaving now, Tony?"

"Yup."

"Thanks for everything." She shook his hand in front of Armand.

"You going for good, Tony?" Armand asked

"No. I'll be back in a week or ten days," he lied. "Why, you gonna miss me?"

Armand laughed. "No, just keeping track of things for Sarah."

"Thanks. Some people are after her so keep an eye out. OK?"

"Yeah, I know, since that incident in the garage. Are they still after her?"

"I think so. I just don't know who or why? It's really frightening to know that someone is out to get you and you haven't the slightest idea who. If you see anything suspicious, tell Sarah."

"Will do." he said. "Flying?"

"Yes. I can't stand train or driving."

"Need a lift to the airport?" Armand asked.

"No, thanks, I'll catch a cab. Bye Sarah."

Tony's Apartment

That afternoon when Tony got to his apartment from LaGuardia airport, he had forgotten the mess that was made when they grabbed him. The door lock was not broken so he assumed they hadn't broken in since he was away. He looked in his bedroom dresser and found the anonymous telephone Sarah gave him. Evidently, no one found it or perhaps didn't even look for it. They came for Sarah but when she wasn't here, they improvised plan B and didn't have time to think about what to do. He went over to his desk and suddenly realized he had left the UPS receipt on Sarah's desk without telling her. It had the tracking number for the hard disk shipment to Alberto. That was a big mistake. He called Sarah. "Hey, Sarah. I forgot to tell you. I left the UPS receipt for the shipment to Alberto on your desk. You should hide or destroy it. I shouldn't have left it."

"Where did you leave it? I didn't see it."

Tony answered, slightly bothered, "Right on top of the desk."

"I'll call you back." She looked all over the desk. "Armand, did you happen to take a UPS receipt that was on my desk?"

"As a matter of fact, yes. When I put the coffee on your desk I saw it. I was going to ask you if you wanted me to track whatever it was." He took it off his desk and handed it to her.

"No, the package already arrived, a gift for the wife of a good friend of mine. I just wanted to see how long it took." She took it into her office, tore it up into tiny pieces and threw them away.

She called Tony right away. "Tony, Armand took the receipt and wanted to know if I wanted him to track it. I got it back and destroyed it."

"That was my mistake," he said. "I'm sorry." Then he thought for a minute. "You know, Sarah, it might just tell us if Armand is somehow involved."

"You're right. But you have to warn Alberto. If they find him it would be dangerous for him and bad for us."

Tony called Alberto and explained what happened.

"That receipt will evidently have my address on it." Alberto was unreasonably calm. "Are you sure this Armand is involved?"

"That's the problem. We don't know. He seems to be very concerned about Sarah but she gets negative vibes about him. In any case, if they now can find you, it might be a tell that he is involved in this affair somehow."

"So my friend. I am now bait, huh? *Cazzo!*" he said with a loud chuckle.

"You know I didn't intend to make you bait. Can you handle it on your end?"

"No problem. *Ghe pensi mi*, Leave it to me." he said in Milanese dialect. "Meanwhile I have good news for you. I have figured out the password for the file."

"Incredible, how did you manage that?"

"I developed an algorithm which has been running on three computers simultaneously for days and it found the password. Now we not only know exactly what is in the file. We can make a file with defective software that won't work but will fool them. and can be used to complete this illicit transaction."

"That's great. You're a prize – on a par with Turing."

"Ha. Think how well Turing would have done with Enigma if he had the computing power I have."

"True," he agreed. "How soon can you get a bad file back into the Amerada account?"

"Two or three hours. I have to be sure the app files I mess up can't be made to work again but good enough to fool them. By tonight they will be in the file. Ti faccio sapere, I'll let you know."

Later that afternoon, two FBI agents arrived to escort Sarah home. "I'm leaving, Armand. These guys are here to make sure I get home OK."

"You didn't have to do that. I would have been glad to take you home."

"Another time," she said. "Someone is trying to obtain my services involuntarily and I don't know who?"

"You going to be OK tonight?"

"I think so," she said.

"You've got my cell phone number," he said. "Call me if you need anything."

"Thanks, Armand. I'll do that. But I don't think there'll be any trouble."

Alberto in Milan

Alberto called the carabiniere barracks. "*Maresciallo Muzzi, per favore.*"

"*Momento.*"

"Muzzi here," the marshall said.

"Maresciallo. This is Alberto DeSanctis. You remember me from the Moffett affair?"

"Of course, Alberto. How are you?"

"Fine thanks. But I may need your help." Alberto told Muzzi as much about the situation as he could without compromising Sarah's secrecy. He asked if Muzzi could, at least for the next couple of days post someone outside his apartment building in case they came after him.

"I can arrange that. In fact I'll send the same officer that saved your ass last time. How's that? He knows you and your apartment."

"That's great, Maresciallo. I appreciate it."

"*Niente.* Glad to help. I'll call in the favor sometime." he said, smiling to himself. "Paolo will be there tonight."

Alberto told Muzzi after the Moffett affair that he would always be available if Muzzi needed him. He called his wife to tell her that he'd be late. Francesca knew Alberto was involved in something important but didn't have any idea what it was. She usually didn't ask and when cases were over, he voluntarily told her the story. She felt a little like Dr. Watson and began to think that maybe she should chronicle his cases.

That Same Evening in DC

Stafford received a phone call. "Yes, Mr. Galahad, It's me."

"Henry, I want you to see if you can get another set of applications for us to make the deal. Time is flying by and we are no closer to finding the file, or even finding out who took it. Ms. Tepper is being very careful and is being protected. Taking her would be very risky, although we are still working on it."

"I can try but as I told you, if I get too pushy, I'll give the whole thing away and jeopardize myself directly. But I'll try."

"Thank you. We don't want to lose this deal."

"Meanwhile, please inform Theodore that I may be accessing the account. As I've said before, I wouldn't want to be an inadvertent casualty of that loose cannon."

"He is not a loose cannon, Henry," Galahad insisted. "He listens carefully to Flint. We had one mistake, true, but that was corrected."

"OK, but see to it please."

"I will. You see what you can do. I am getting very concerned. I'm afraid our buyer will back out of the deal. It's not life or death to them. It is almost that for us."

Henry took some cold chicken from his fridge, put it on a plate and added some cole slaw. He missed the dinners that his divorce removed from his life. He poured himself some white wine, turned on the TV and sat down to eat. When he finished, he neatly put the dishes in the dishwasher and sat down at his computer. Before he did anything to obtain a new set of apps, he retrieved the Amerada account just to see if he could still access it.

To his surprise, he saw the missing file. It suddenly appeared and Stafford had no idea how. Maybe it was never missing, he thought. Something was fishy. He tried to open it but couldn't The file was apparently encrypted and he didn't know the password so he couldn't open it. Instead of calling Mr. Galahad, he immediately called Yuri.

"Yuri, Henry. The file has mysteriously reappeared."

"Really? How could that happen?"

"I have no idea but it's there and it's encrypted."

How do you know it's real?" Yuri asked.

"I'm not sure but the fact that it's encrypted is a good sign. You have the password, don't you?"

"I got one at the deal that died."

"What is it? I can try it."

"Hang on a minute. It's KingArthur1300. Upper case K and A."

"Let me try it. Wait." Stafford said. He typed in the password and the file opened up. "Eureka," he said. "It opened. It must be real. I will send it to you. Is the money still available?"

"Of course," Yuri answered.

"Put my share in my Swiss account and I'll send it to you."

"You send it first, Henry."

"I won't do that Yuri. I have no leverage if you renege. You have leverage."

"What leverage?" Yuri asked.

"I know what your government can do to me if it wants to. I can't look over my shoulder all my life. I have no such resource."

"All right. I'll send the money. I won't have access to the cash until tomorrow."

"As soon as I see the money in my account, I'll email the file to you."

"Fair enough. Until tomorrow then."

Galahad reacts

"Herman, this is Galahad. Tell Theodore that Stafford may be accessing Amerada. I have authorized it."

"Mr. Galahad. Theodore just told me Stafford already entered the account and that there is a file in the account and it is encrypted."

"Does he think it's the real one?"

"Yes, he does."

"Where did it come from?" Galahad asked.

"He doesn't know. He just went into the account this evening, just to check and was surprised and puzzled to see the file. He has no idea where it came from or how it got into the account. Didn't Stafford tell you?"

"No, he didn't. Let me call you back." Galahad answered. He immediately placed a call to Stafford. "Henry, Theodore is now aware of your entry. Did you find anything of consequence?"

"No. I was just seeing if I could get into the account. The password hasn't changed." "

Did you see anything, per chance, that we might have missed about where the file went?"

"Unfortunately, no."

"Galahad frowned with his reaction to Stafford's comment. OK. Keep in touch with me regarding your progress in obtaining another set of applications." Galahad was becoming very angry. Henry must know that the file is there and that it's encrypted. Why didn't he tell me? Has he made his own deal? Galahad called Yuri.

"Hello. This is Yuri Malenkov."

"Yuri, it's me. We need a few more days before we close."

"My government is now suggesting that they may want to back out of the deal. They will give me a firm answer in two days."

"Why would they want to back out?"

"I don't know. I told them that it's a bad idea to back out, but they said they would let me know. I can't understand it."

"Fine. Let me know." Galahad called Flint back. "Herman. Tell Theodore to do his thing on Stafford's computer."

"Stafford? You sure?"

"I am convinced that Stafford is trying to cross us. He has found the file and didn't tell me. Why? And our buyer is suggesting that the government may back out of the deal. The only sensible reason to back out is that they are getting the same merchandise elsewhere."

"You sure about this?" Flint asked.

"I'm sure enough. In fact, I have a better idea, neater. Wait for my call. I'll call Stafford and confront him. Then I'll be sure. If I'm right, I have to stop him before he sends the file to the buyer. I worry because I gave the buyer the encryption password before the deal aborted. If he gets the file, he will save the 300 million and keep it for himself and whoever else is in this with him.

Galahad called Stafford. "Stafford, here."

"Henry, We know the file reappeared. Why didn't you tell me?"

Stafford answered quickly, "I didn't know it. I just discovered it when you called."

"We know you had already been in the account when I called you earlier. You must have seen the file. I'll ask you again. Why didn't you let me know?"

"I didn't think there was any rush," Stafford answered. Galahad hung up angrily and called Flint.

"I was right, Herman. Tell Theodore to save the file onto his computer immediately and delete it from the Amerada account. Quickly, please."

"All right. I'll call you back."

Sarah's apartment

Sarah was frightened. She was not used to this kind of pressure and couldn't relax. She poured herself a glass of white wine and called Tony. She got no answer. She tried again with no luck. Then she realized he may be on a plane. There would be no service. About twenty minutes later, Tony called her. "Just landed."

"Am I glad to hear your voice. I was worried. I didn't know you were flying and there wasn't any answer on your phone. After the last incident, I take nothing for granted."

"Sorry. I guess I should have told you. In any case, I should be at your apartment in about half an hour. Is everything OK?"

"Seems so. My FBI escort got me home OK. Since Alberto put an encrypted file in the Amerada account, they probably think they have what they need, so perhaps they've stopped looking for me."

"Could be. If they have the merchandise, they don't need you. In any case, we can talk when I get there."

No sooner did Tony arrive at Sarah's, when Alberto called on Tony's phone.

"Tony, just to inform you. The doctored file I inserted has been deleted from the Amerada account. I think it was done by the same computer that did the killing. The computer isn't in the same place it was. It now appears to be in D.C. proper."

"Do you know where?" Tony asked.

"I can't pinpoint it. I admit, I haven't tried very hard. I've been busy at my job and my spare time was taken up by creating harmless applications for the file."

"That's too bad, but I'm not complaining. The FBI went to the last location and was too late. He had already skipped out. If you have the time, see what you can find out."

"Sure. Just that there's not enough time in the day. Francesca is beginning to complain."

Tony laughed. "Ah, the chains of marriage. Do what you can. You've already done more than I could have hoped. Ciao."

"Ciao, saluti alla Sarah."

"He sends you his regards. He called to say the file was deleted from the account by the killer computer. He can't pinpoint it except to say it's in D.C. proper. He's been too busy to track it down."

"I've got to get some sleep," she said. "I assume you're going to crash here tonight."

"Of course, you need protection," he said, smiling.

"You sure that's not self-serving?" She raised her eyebrow.

"Of course it is." He put his arms around her and kissed her.

"It's about that time," she whispered, and kissed him again. "My bed is big enough for the two of us." It had been a long time for both of them.

CHAPTER XIV

May 22nd

Stafford checked his bank account on-line. The money had still not been deposited. Before he called Yuri to push him, he checked the Amerada account. The file was gone. "Shit, shit, shit," he mumbled to himself. "I knew I should have downloaded it. Damn. Damn!" he repeated pounding his desk. His anger at himself turned to panic. He knew Galahad suspected something so Stafford was hoping to get his money and disappear as fast as possible. Now he didn't know what Galahad would do and didn't know how Yuri would react when he told him. He thought briefly about waiting for the money and then disappearing without telling Yuri. But he knew the Russian FSB would eventually find him and they are not merciful in how they kill you.

He began to pace. He did not know what to do. Eventually, he concluded that he had to make up two stories, one for Yuri which would be the truth and one for Galahad to save his neck and maybe his share of the sale. After mulling things over, he called Galahad. "This is Henry Stafford. I was not truthful with you, Mr. Galahad."

"How so, Henry?"

"I was threatened by Yuri Malenkov. I have some things in my past that are better kept secret. He found out about them and was threatening to release the information and ruin my career with NSA if I didn't help him. When I saw the file I thought I was out of danger. But I can't go through with it."

"What would you like me to do?"

"I downloaded a copy of the file onto my computer. When I went to delete it from the Amerada account, I found it missing. I panicked. I knew Yuri had the password."

"How did you know that?" Galahad asked.

"Yuri told me. He offered me money to get a copy of the file for him. His plan was to keep the money for himself and pay me a sum for the file."

"I see. And what are your plans, Henry?"

"I cannot go ahead with it. I've made up my mind that his threat is only a bluff and if I work at it, I can counteract what he divulges with an excuse. If you need a copy of the file, I have it," he lied.

Galahad didn't know whether to believe him or not. The story seemed plausible. He would give him another chance. It could only cost him some money. "Destroy the file, Henry. I wouldn't want it to fall into Yuri's hands accidentally. It would be an expensive accident." Now Galahad knew why Yuri was delaying. He wanted to keep the ball in the air until he was sure he could get the file from Stafford and be sure that it was the real merchandise.

Stafford was relieved. He had no file to destroy. His bluff with Galahad worked, at least he hoped so. He called Yuri. "It's me. I want you to hold the money. I do not have the file."

"What? What happened?"

"When I went into the account, it was missing again. And stupid me, I didn't make a copy for myself. I have no idea what happened but I no longer can provide it."

"That's very strange. You think someone erased it?"

"I have no idea. I only know it's not there. I don't know how it reappeared either."

"That's too bad. But thank you for telling me. If something should happen and the file comes back, call me, fast. But for now I have to arrange to do the deal." Yuri was angry but at least he would get something. He would get a 10% fee from the Kremlin which was nothing to ignore. It would have been a huge amount if he got the file himself.

Sarah's office

Sarah came to work with Tony who left her at the elevator in the lobby of her building. He did not want anyone in her office to know he was in town. He had arranged with Alberto that they would try to pinpoint the killer computer. When Sarah came into the NSA office, everyone looked at her. Armand stood up when she passed his desk. "You OK?"

"Why is everyone looking at me as if I'm back from the dead?"

"Rumors and gossip."

"What do they think happened?"

"I have no idea. I just hear whispering. You ever going to tell me what did really happen? I don't listen to gossip. It's usually way off."

"I'd rather not go into details. There's something funny going on with this Amerada account and until I find out what, I'm jumpy."

"May I ask what kind of funny?"

Sarah decided to tell him something. Otherwise, he would hear things that would usually be so far off as to be dangerous. "The account was passworded and no one knew anything about the account. When I was finally able to get into the account, there was a mysterious file encrypted in the account with a password."

"How did you get into the account?" he asked.

"That, I think, is what got Hugo Barnhill killed. He was trying to get into the account for me."

"So how did you get in?" he asked, showing genuine interest.

"I have other resources that worked." she intentionally was vague. "The mysterious file disappeared, then reappeared and then disappeared again. I have no clue what's going on," she lied. "But I'm getting closer."

"This Amerada account, it's an NSA account. Do you know who's involved here?"

"I have heavy suspicions but I can't prove anything, yet."

"Who is it? Maybe if I know who you are onto, I can keep my ears open. I talk to people."

"I'd rather not say, Armand. I have someone working on the forensics and as soon as I can prove it, we'll move in. I don't want to scare him off."

"I have my own idea," he said. "I'm quietly observant and since that episode in the garage, I nose around more than usual."

"Really? Who do you think?" She was truly surprised at his comment.

"I may be wrong but somehow, I think Henry Stafford was behaving strangely."

Sarah wasn't surprised to hear that. Everyone at NSA is nosey to the point of paranoia. His odd behavior with the Amerada account and my emails must have been noticeable to others beside herself. "I agree with you. In fact, I have Bill Armitage checking him out. But I don't think he's alone in whatever is transpiring. So far I have nothing firm. I need proof."

"Maybe I can get it for you," he said.

Her ears perked up and she sat back in her chair. "And just how do you think you can do that?"

He smiled. "Remember, I work at NSA. I have my resources."

Sarah laughed. She wondered was there really a possibility that Armand could get the proof she needed to nail Henry. And what about this man Flint; or the hooded mystery man Tony told her about, the one who questioned him when he was kidnapped? Should she mention the name to him or not? Listening to Armand, she felt better about him but not enough to let him in on what she already knew. "OK. Any help would certainly be appreciated."

Galahad

"Yuri, I have the merchandise. When can we make the deal?" Galahad asked.

"Anytime you are ready. The money is now in a bank and can be transferred."

"Transfer the money to my Swiss account which I will text to you. As soon as I receive the money, I will transfer the file to you. You already have the password to decrypt it."

"You have always been a man of your word. I do it reluctantly because it is an enormous sum but for you I will do it. Watch for it this afternoon."

"I shall. Is the email address I have for you still valid?" Galahad asked.

"Yes, it still is."

"OK then everything is a go. Goodbye for now."

Galahad called Flint. "Herman, Yuri is making a transfer to my account. When the total sum is there, I will call you and you will have Theodore transfer the file to Yuri to the address we have on file. I also would like you to think about what we should do about Stafford. When we speak later, you can give me your suggestion."

"I will await your call."

Sarah

Sarah and Tony were having lunch at a small cafe near the office. "Now we wait. I assume the transfer will be made soon and then when they try the apps," her voice trailed off, she made a symbolic explosion with her hands and added, "Poof."

Armitage joined them at Sarah's request. After the greetings, Sarah said, "Bill, I expect that the sale will now go through. My techie made sure the apps appeared to be effective but as soon as they are tried, it will become obvious that they are fraudulent and, I might add, not fixable."

"Then over the next few days, I should be monitoring what I can; phones, emails, large bank transfers and anything else that will help."

"Did you ever find anything out about this guy Flint?" Tony asked.

"I have a picture of him, that's all I have so far,"

"If you have it with you, may I see it?" Tony said. Bill took the photo from his pocket and put it on the table. "Yup, that's the guy that questioned me. The other guy kept his hood on so I never saw his face. But he carried himself in a distinct way.

"How was that?"

"I can't describe it but if I saw him move, I think I would recognize him. Also, his voice was almost a whisper as if to disguise it."

"Has anyone given you any trouble?" Bill asked Sarah.

"Not since we produced the file in the Amerada account. It seems reasonable they only wanted me to get the missing file. I suspect that after the sale is made and the apps are tested, the shit will hit the fan and I'll have to watch my ass."

"You're probably right," Tony said. "That's why we need a heads up on when the transfer is made." Looking at Armitage, "I'm hoping your monitoring effort will give us the notice we need."

They had finished lunch and as Tony was paying the check, his phone rang. "Tony, *sono Alberto. Ti do una notizia. Il movimento del file e' stato fatto.*"

"*Grazie, amico, ciao.* The file has been transferred," Tony told Sarah and Bill. Now we wait for the explosion."

"I guess I better get on it right away. Talk to you later." Bill walked away with spring in his step. Sarah and Tony walked slowly and Tony let Sarah leave him at the entrance to her building.

"Call me when you get a chance," he said.

"See you later. I assume we go to my place together when I leave."

"You got it. Call me when you're ready to leave and I'll meet you at your car in the garage. Bye." He gave her a peck on the cheek.

Galahad

"Herman, now that the transaction has been completed, we need to discuss Stafford," Galahad said.

"I suspected that was coming. What do you want to do about him? I don't think he deserves anything, considering he tried to screw us."

"The way I see it, Herman, we have two choices. We either give him his share, distasteful as that may seem or..." There was a long pause causing Flint to be impatient.

"Or what?"

"We eliminate him, permanently," Galahad replied.

There was silence on both sides of the phone for several interminable seconds. "I'm not happy about killing him," Flint said. "Too dangerous. I'm not ready to risk life in prison."

"What about Barnhill? It's not as if we are pure, Herman."

"They can't pin that on us. It would be very difficult. But if we do it again, we are taking a risk. Besides, you have remained anonymous. The New York policeman we apprehended has seen me. He can identify me. We expected to eliminate him and you know what happened."

"Is it worth giving Stafford seventy-five million dollars to keep him quiet?" Galahad answered his own question. "I don't think so. I suggest you have Theodore do what he does. If you are worried, you can take your share and disappear."

"All right. I will do it. When do we split the money?"

"As soon as Yuri says he is satisfied. If he is not, I must return the money. I don't want to accidentally drink something radioactive. You know how the Russians behave."

"Against my better judgement, I am trusting you."

Galahad laughed. "Herman, I do have a reputation to uphold."

"How do I know you won't kill me as well?"

"I am not a greedy man, Herman. My reason for killing Stafford is that he is greedy and was willing to cut us out for more money. Despite what you have heard, there is honor among thieves. You have my word that as soon as Yuri says OK, I will pay off everyone. I don't want to spend the rest of my life worrying."

"All right, Mr. Galahad. I'll have Theodore do his thing. Tell me, will I ever find out who you are?"

"Perhaps, perhaps. Goodbye Herman. Call me when it is done."

Herman hailed a cab and went to the obscure office where Theodore had set himself up after leaving Arlington. When he entered the office, he found Theodore doing what he always does, looking at a computer screen. "Theodore, I want you to send your e-missive to Henry Stafford."

"What? Why? He is on our team, isn't he?"

"He was. He tried to make the deal without us."

"Why would he do that?"

"Greed, Theodore, Greed. As soon as the customer is satisfied, the money will be distributed and you will get your share. And it will be larger now that one share is being eliminated."

"I will set it up now and then watch for the result. But it probably won't happen until he gets home later. I don't want to send it to his office computer. Someone else might access it accidentally."

"Fine. I'll leave you. Call me when you know the result."

"OK, Mr. Flint." He went back to watching his computer screen and began typing as Flint was leaving.

Later That Evening

Henry Stafford had finished his dinner at his usual haunt, a local diner near his apartment. He paid the check and walked home in the windless evening. The first thing he did was to pour himself a tumbler of scotch and sat down at the TV set for the news on CNN.

He called Galahad. "Where does the deal stand?"

"It's been concluded," Galahad answered flatly.

"When will you be paying out?" he asked.

"As soon as the buyer gives me the OK that the merchandise is what he purchased."

"Why wait for that?"

"Because if he has complaints, I will refund his money. I gave him my word," Galahad replied. "Why are you asking, Henry? Do you think you deserve anything?"

"What?" Stafford asked. "If you're joking, it's not funny."

Galahad answered, still with no expression in his voice, "I'm not joking, Henry. You tried to make a deal yourself without us. Unfortunately for you, it failed. And now you want your share of a deal you tried to beat us out of. You can't play both sides, Henry. You lost."

"That's preposterous," Stafford answered. "Why would you say something like that? Trying to cut me out?"

"No Henry, you cut yourself out with your greed and duplicity. Good night, Henry."

"You pull that on me, Galahad, and you'll be very sorry. I'll bring the walls down on you."

"Good night, Henry." He hung up.

"Galahad, Galahad," he yelled into the phone, then slammed it down and took a gulp of his scotch. What should he do, he wondered. He needed the money and now he dug a hole for himself because he wanted a bigger share. He called Yuri.

"Why are you calling me so late, Henry? It's almost morning, here."

"Galahad knows we tried to double-cross him. Now he's cutting me out and I need the money."

"What do you expect me to do? I lost a very large sum because you couldn't deliver."

"I need some money, Yuri. You owe me that."

"I agree that you did try to help me but that was self-serving. My fee from the government is nowhere near the sum we would have cashed in if you had gotten me the file."

"I deserve something, even it if failed. You have to come across with something."

Yuri answered, "I'll see what I can do. I'll call you after I get my fee."

"Thanks, I appreciate that, Yuri. Good night." Stafford hung up the phone without waiting for an answer. He took another gulp of his scotch and sat down at his computer to check his email. At first, he didn't notice the hum. Then as it grew louder, the realization suddenly came to him. "Theodore," he said out loud. The plug, the plug he thought, where is the outlet?

CHAPTER XV

May 23rd

Tony felt that Sarah was safe, at least for the moment, so he opted to return to New York. His boss was sympathetic allowing him to stay in D.C. when Tony explained what was happening.

Sarah drove him to the station to catch an early train and then went to her office. It was too early for Armand to be in the office. Something about an empty office seemed calming. She thought it might not be a bad idea to make a habit of getting to the office early, starting her day feeling good.

Instinctively, she looked over her desk to see if anything was out of place. She always did. As best she could tell, everything was just as she left it. She called Tony as she promised to tell him she was all right and as soon as she hung up, Bill Armitage came into her office.

"Armand not here?" he asked as he closed the door behind him.

"Too early for him. But you're in early. "What's up?"

"Henry Stafford's dead. They found him last night."

Sarah perked up. "How? What happened?" she asked with shock and some apprehension in her voice.

"Police came when several tenants called 911 about an explosion in the building. His computer exploded."

"Another one? Like Barnhill?"

"Exactly like Barnhill and the near miss you had with Manson."

"Where is his computer now?"

"The police have it."

"Any possibility we can get it? national security reason?" she added as an excuse. "If we can get something out of the hard drive, it might get us closer to whoever's doing all this.

"I'll try. I would especially like to check his email on the hard drive if it's salvageable."

"What's your take on why this happened?" Sarah asked him.

"I can only speculate, Sarah. I really don't know."

"What do you think? Give me your best guess.

"Well, if you remember, there were two people looking for you in New York, on the same day and at almost the same time. Something as well organized as this Amerada caper wouldn't have two people looking for you at the same time, separately. Doesn't make sense."

"So, what does that mean?"

"The only thing I can come up with is that there were two competing entities for the same deal. Flint and Stafford. I don't know the relationship between them but it would seem the Flint people, whoever they are, killed Stafford."

Armand knocked on her door and stuck his head in. "You guys want some coffee?"

"Thanks Armand, bring us two. How do you take it Bill?"

"Just milk."

"Just milk for Bill," she repeated.

"Got it," Armand said. "Back soon."

"How do you feel about him?"

"He's been great lately. There seems to be a side of him he never showed me. Maybe he's just shy and it's taken a while for him to loosen up."

"That's good. I feel better with him around and aware of the situation. How much does he know?"

"Only what he's found out himself through what he calls 'his sources.' I haven't added to his knowledge. I'm not ready to do that."

"I'll tell him about Stafford. I think he should be aware."

"I'll agree to that much. Meanwhile let me know what you find out from the police."

Armitage got up to leave.

"Aren't you going to stay for your coffee? Armand will be back with it in a couple of minutes."

He sat back down. "I forgot. So help me, I think I'm getting old." He laughed.

"Why should you be any different?"

Sarah picked up the ringing phone. "Tepper. Oh hi Boss. (pause) yes it's true. The same way as yours and Barnhill. We have no clue yet, only unsupported ideas. I'll drop up to see you in a while and tell you what I know. Bill Armitage is here. He's the one who told me about it. Talk to you later, Bye."

Armand brought the coffee in and put it down on Sarah's desk. Armitage said. "Just so you know. Henry Stafford was killed last night. Computer blew up."

"My God. This thing doesn't seem to end. How?"

"Don't know, yet. That's the mystery."

"Any idea who did it?"

"Not yet. But we'll find out. Meanwhile, keep an eye on Sarah. We don't know if she's in any danger."

"I will certainly do so. I knew something serious was going on since the episode in the garage but Sarah wouldn't tell me what it was about. It's this Amerada thing that's been rumored around, isn't it?"

"Yes it is. But I can't tell you any more than that."

Armand left the office and Armitage said, "He seems like he's in your corner."

"Seems so. But regarding Amerada, I'll still keep my own counsel."

"That's fine. As long as he watches out for you. Thanks for the coffee, but I've a lot to do, as you can imagine. Take care." He got up to leave. "Keep an eye out," he said to Armand as he walked by his desk.

Sarah left her office and told Armand, "Going up to 12 to tell Manson what happened. Back in about a half hour."

Sarah ordered her lunch in. She was concerned about leaving the office alone. She had no idea when the buyer of the file would find out the apps contained in it don't work. At that point, she felt she would be a target to find the real file. She had no idea how much money was involved but she assumed it had to be a large amount to involve four killings that she knew of.

Milan

Alberto came into his apartment after having wolfed down a panino and orangina at the coffee bar up the street. He immediately called Sarah.

"Sarah, this is Alberto. I was wondering is there any reason I should keep this file? It seems to me that I should delete it now that we know what's in it and have a non-working copy."

"There's nothing in the file that could be used as evidence, is there?"

"I can't imagine. Especially since we've done all kinds of things to the Amerada account. The account itself might have been used in some way as evidence if it were untouched. But then we wouldn't have found anything out."

"True. The best thing is to destroy it. As long as it exists, it's a security risk for us."

"OK. I'll do that right away. Meanwhile, I have been monitoring this guy Wintervale's computer to pick up on anything that indicates the deal has gone bad."

"That's a good idea. We're watching what we can here as well."

"Good. *Stai attento, Ciao.*"

As far as the Amerada affair is concerned, Alberto felt there was nothing to do but wait for the proverbial shit to hit the fan. He looked at his watch. Where was Francesca? She went to visit her sister but should have been back by now. Just as he had that thought, he heard the big iron gate in the courtyard open and looked out his back window in time to see his car going down to the garage. He felt better. Since the Moffett affair he worries about her every time he puts himself at risk, afraid she will be used against him. Besides, he really misses her when she's not home. He heard the footsteps and met her at the door. He took the shopping bags out of her hands, hugged her with one arm, patting her swollen belly with the other. "*Mi mancavi tanto. Come va la Marcella?*"

"*Bene. Si tira avanti. Hai mangato, caro?*"

"*Si, un panino.*"

She laughed. "*Panino? Peccato!*"

Later in DC

That evening, Galahad received a call from Yuri. "Tell me, are there written instructions that go with these apps? We are having difficulty using them and considering how much we paid, that's the least you can provide."

"Those apps are internally self-documented. There's a link button in the upper left hand corner to a help screen."

"It's there, but the software is not doing what it's supposed to do. I hope you provide technical support," Yuri spoke somewhat brusquely.

"I will be happy to do so."

"Good, I will come with my technical guy."

"When will you come?"

"I just arrived in the U.S. I'm already at our U.N. office in New York. I can be there in the morning. Is that all right?"

"That's fine. I can't meet you myself. Call me when you get to Washington and I'll tell you where to go and who to see. Is that OK?"

"That works. We should be there late morning, allowing for city traffic on both ends. I'll let you know how it works out."

"Talk to you tomorrow, Yuri. Goodnight." He called Theodore immediately. "Theodore, our buyer is complaining that the apps don't work properly and that maybe he is doing something wrong. He is coming tomorrow to get help. Have you tried the apps yourself?"

"No, I haven't. But I shouldn't have any trouble figuring them out and helping him. When is he coming?"

"Late morning. I will send him over to you. Meanwhile, get yourself up to speed so you can provide the help he needs. I don't need any more trouble. I don't need to tell you what's at stake here."

"I'll do that. Do you want me to call you when they are comfortable with the apps?"

"Not necessary. I'm sure they will. Good night Theodore." He poured himself a glass of orange juice and sat down to watch the news on TV. After about ten minutes he dozed off on the couch. He did not know how long he slept when the ringing phone woke him. "Hello."

"Mr. Galahad. This is Theodore. We have trouble. The apps don't work."

"What do you mean they don't work?"

"Just what I said. They indeed are self-explanatory. And the instructions are very clear and easy to follow. The apps don't work."

"Did you try them all?" Galahad asked.

"Yes, all of them. None of them does what they are supposed to do."

Galahad thought for a minute. The missing file that suddenly appeared, he thought. It must have been doctored in some way. But who did it and how? Tepper, we must find out from her. He called Flint. "Herman, we have trouble."

"What trouble?"

"Yuri complained that the apps don't work and is coming here for tech support. Theodore claims Yuri is right. The apps don't work."

"What can we do? The file with all the apps was there."

"True, but remember the file disappeared mysteriously and just as mysteriously reappeared. They must have been doctored."

"Who?" Flint asked.

"I don't know. Our original plan to get Sarah Tepper must be implemented. She is the only one that would know what's going on. No one else is working on the Amerada affair. We must get hold of Sarah Tepper and make her tell us who did this. We must get those apps or I will have to return all of the money. I will leave it to you to grab her and take her to our place in the district. Make sure she is hooded until she gets there. I would hate to have to eliminate her."

"I will try to arrange it."

"Don't try, Herman, do it, and soon." Galahad called Yuri. "Do not make your trip tomorrow."

"Why not?"

"The apps do not work. The difficulty you are having is not your fault. Something is wrong and I need some more time to find out what happened."

Yuri answered testily. "We are running out of patience. I will give you some more time but not too much. If you don't resolve the situation fairly soon, my government will cancel the deal. A word to the wise, they say."

Galahad was trying to avoid panic. He doesn't think clearly under that kind of stress. The whole deal was in danger of being kiboshed. He was well aware that there was no reason for Yuri to back out. If Yuri did, he would lose his ten percent fee for obtaining the apps. "Not to worry," Galahad answered, calmly "We will get it resolved soon. Thank you for your patience."

"Goodbye, remember, not too much time."

"Goodbye."

Later

Tony answered the call from Alberto. Alberto told him that something was happening, that the Wintervale computer was accessing the files. As best Alberto could tell, if Wintervale was accessing the files, he must be testing them. This meant to both of them that they had already discovered the problem. "I have to warn Sarah. I'll call you back." Tony called Sarah several times with no answer. He could only imagine the worst. He called Armitage to tell he that Sarah was not answering her phone and he was worried.

"I'll send some agents to her house," Armitage said. "I'll call you back as soon as I hear." Tony called Alberto. "Alberto, I think we were too late. If they have her, that means we have double trouble. She might be forced to tell them where to find you."

"Don't worry about me, I have enough protection. I am trying to find the Wintervale computer. It's a good bet that if she's been taken, that's where they would take her. Let me work. I'll call you if I can locate it. Keep in touch."

Sarah captive

Sarah was frightened. She had a hood over her head which made it worse. She had been sitting tied to a chair with her hands bound for over a half hour. She was sure she was still in the district since the car ride only took ten minutes. She mentally berated herself for opening the apartment door. She had let her guard down since putting the file back in the Amerada account. She was warned that the threat was imminent as soon as they discovered the files didn't work. She just wasn't thinking. She didn't have the paranoid instinct that a covert agent has. She was only a desk jockey she told herself.

With the hood still over her head, she was asked, "Where is the Amerada file, Sarah?"

Sarah did not answer. She knew the file no longer existed. She and Alberto had decided to erase it. It was risky to leave it out there to be stolen again. But what should she tell them? If she told them it had been erased, they might just kill her since she was of no use to them. She did not know who was holding her and suddenly realized the hood over her head might just save her life. She decided to tell them the truth because it would be believable. They would spot a lie. They weren't stupid.

"Sarah," he repeated. "Don't make things difficult. Tell me where the file is or you will surely be very sorry. We have ways to make you tell us but you really don't want us to use them. Please believe me."

Sarah's fear had abated quite a bit, replaced with anger at her situation. She answered them calmly, "As soon as we were able to get into the Amerada account, we found the encrypted file. After several days, we succeeded in breaking the encryption password. At that point, we doctored the apps and replaced the file with doctored apps back in the Amerada account, properly encrypted. The original file with the real apps in it was erased. It is no longer available. You lose."

"I don't believe you," he said quietly.

She continued, "Once we opened the file and could access the apps, and learned the encryption password, there was no reason to keep the file. It was a security risk out there, so we erased it. NSA has the apps. We own them."

"You must get them for us," Flint said.

"I personally don't have access to the apps and it would be impossible to get another copy of each. They would arrest me on the spot. I have no right to have them. How did you get them in the first place?"

One of the men looked at the other and said quietly, "Tell her."

"Henry Stafford obtained them for us."

"Stafford is dead. Who killed him?" she asked.

"That is not your business," the man answered.

"I'll assume one of you did it. My question is why?"

"His greed," he answered. "He tried to make the deal without us."

Sarah had begun to feel in control of herself and sense that she had the upper hand in the situation. They obviously were in trouble with the apps not available. Without them there was no deal. "I don't know who you are but we have reached an impossible stalemate. I cannot get the file that was in the Amerada account since it no longer exists. The apps are only available on the NSA server which is very tightly controlled. As I have already told you, I cannot just take the files. And as you well know," she said sarcastically, "Stafford is no longer in a condition to get them again nor at the very least tell me how he managed it. So, as I see it, you are plain and simply fucked. Since I don't know who you are, your best option is to cut your losses, let me go and if you lay low, you may get lucky and stay out of jail."

One of the men nodded to the other and without saying anything, they untied her from the chair, kept her bound and hooded and, one on each arm, they led her.

"Where are you taking me?" she asked. They did not answer. She repeated it louder. "Where are you taking me?" trying to free herself from the arms holding her. They persisted, eventually forcing her into the back seat of a car, still bound and hooded.

CHAPTER XVI

May 24th

Tony called Armitage. "Bill, Sarah has still not answered her phone. My techie says that the killer computer is trying out the apps which can only mean they have discovered the truth about them. I am worried that they have taken her."

"I'll try to get some agents or the police to her apartment. Call you back as soon as I get some information. Have you any idea where this fucking computer is?"

"No, not yet. We are trying to pinpoint it. Please call me when you know something about Sarah. I'm catching the next plane down there. I should be there in the wee hours. If you don't get me, I'm probably in the air."

Tony took a cab right to the airport. He caught the 12:30 plane which left ten minutes late but got him to Washington and to Sarah's apartment by 2:15 a.m. When he got to Sarah's apartment, there was a small crowd in front of her building. Tony forced his way through and saw Sarah sitting on the sidewalk with a policeman hovering over her and a woman talking to her. "How is she?" he asked.

Sarah looked up when she heard Tony's voice. "Tony" She reached up for him and he picked her up to stand and she hugged him and wouldn't let him go.

"You know this woman?" the policeman asked.

"Yes, I came because I was worried about her."

The woman said, "I'm a nurse. She was apparently dropped on the sidewalk in front of the building, bound and with a hood over her head."

He pushed her back to talk. "Are you hurt Sarah?" he asked.

"No, not really. I'm a little bruised because they literally pushed me out of the car onto the sidewalk. I was lying there fifteen minutes before someone stopped to see what was wrong. Then the police came."

"OK. Let's get up to your apartment." He looked at the nurse and the policeman. "I can take her from here. But I would like to know your name. We really appreciate what you did."

"I'm Anna Moreno. I work at George Washington University Hospital, children's ward. I was on my way to work."

"Thanks, Anna. I assume I can find you there."

"Yes, you can. I'm glad she's OK."

Tony asked the stocky policeman if he wanted to come up to the apartment. "Not necessary, she told me what happened and since she's NSA, better if we make light of it for now. Someone may call you from the station tomorrow, or should I say later this morning for a statement. Sarah gave me her name and phone number." Anna and the policeman stood there and watched with the small crowd as Tony led Sarah into the building.

When they entered the apartment, Tony was a little surprised. "Did you put up a fight?"

"I struggled but they were too strong and put the hood over my head. They didn't even come into the apartment. They just dragged me right from the doorway."

"Did you recognize them?" Tony asked.

"No. There were two, both big and strong. I had never seen them before."

"Do you think you could recognize them from a photo?" He asked.

"I think so."

Tony convinced Sarah to get some sleep and when she awoke, they would go to the police station to make a statement and perhaps look at photos to identify her kidnappers. She went right to bed and was out in minutes. Tony decided to sleep on a living room chair. He had napped on the flight so he wasn't too sleepy. His mind was working to figure out what would happen next. The deal which didn't go through was probably worth a great deal so it wasn't likely they would give up too easily. If, as Sarah told him, Stafford was their source for the apps and he's gone, the logical next choice was Sarah. This might explain why they let her go. They intend to use her again. But how? She told them she couldn't just take them without getting arrested. She didn't know how Stafford accomplished it without exposing himself.

Maybe her kidnappers knew how Stafford did it and will eventually ask Sarah to reproduce the event. But it would have to be a threat. What kind of threat? Tony's mind was racing but could not come to any conclusion. Eventually he nodded off and was in a deep sleep when Sarah awakened him with a kiss on his forehead.

"Want some breakfast, sleepyhead?"

Tony awoke with a start. For a second, he didn't realize where he was. He smiled at Sarah. "Sure, watcha got?"

"Coffee and a cinnamon bun. That enough?"

"Breakfast for an Italian, it's overeating. For me, a cappuccino with nothing is enough."

"Sorry, you'll have to do with plain old Chock Full-o-Nuts."

An hour later, Tony had washed his face and freshened himself up. He had slept with his clothes on. "Sarah, I think we should meet with Armitage before we go to the police. I'm concerned about what will happen next."

Sarah looked at him, said nothing, and called Bill Armitage. "Bill, Tony wants a meeting. You available?" She listened and said "What? The White House? What did you tell them? OK see you then."

"OK, He's free about 10:30. That OK?"

"Great. What was that about the White House?"

"National security office called. They had heard about things."

Tony looked at his watch. "If we grab a cab, we can get there just in time. Let's go"

Armitage's Office

"You wanted this meeting, Tony. Shoot." Armitage said.

"Bill, this isn't over. They let Sarah go for a reason. I can only speculate why. But everything I come up with as a possible reason is not good. The most logical reason is that they want to use her to get the files again. But I can't imagine how. The other is that they believe the Amerada file has been erased and they want to use her to get the five apps that were in the file."

"Whatever they do," Tony, "I'm sure they're in a hurry. They don't have time to wait too long on a deal like this."

"That's what worries me. Whatever they do, it's going to be an all or nothing "Hail Mary" pass. And if that doesn't work God knows what will come next. They are killers and evidently have a lot at stake."

Sarah listened and said nothing. She looked back and forth between Armitage and Tony like a tennis match. They adjourned after an hour discussion, having decided the next step.

"I want to go to my office, Tony. I can't believe they've done nothing. There has got to be some kind of message."

"You're probably right. I'll go with you."

Theodore

Theodore was sitting at his computer looking at the screen and said. "It's true, Mr. Flint. Stafford's access has not been cancelled yet."

"Can you get into the NSA server and get the files?"

"No, unfortunately. I don't know his password."

"Can't you get it, somehow?"

"With time, there's a good chance. But I can't do it as fast as you want."

Flint called Galahad. "He can't get in. He needs Stafford's password. No, he says it will take time which we don't have. I agree. I think we can do both. Yes, I have the address. Bye."

Flint made another call. "Yes, it's Flint. I want you to go ahead with what we discussed. I will text you the address in Milan, Italy. His name is DeSanctis. Thank you. And time is of the essence."

He made another call. "Yes leave the message in the mailbox of her apartment house as soon as you can. Yes, the one I gave you yesterday. Theodore, I will be in touch. See if you can get the password while we are trying other avenues."

"OK Mr. Flint, I'll do the best I can."

Flint put on his hat and left. When he got to the street, he called Galahad. "It's been done. I hope so, too." He hung up and stopped walked to the corner to catch a bus.

That afternoon

Sarah spent the afternoon in her office thinking. She got nothing done and regarding Amerada, she had no idea what to do and what might happen next. Armand knocked on her door and stuck his head in. "You OK, Sarah?"

She looked up and him and said nothing.

"Anything you want me to do?"

"No, thanks Armand. I think everything is under control. I just have to wait."

"Wait for what?"

"Just wait. I have no idea for what. Just wait," she repeated, "until the situation plays itself out."

"That sounds very mysterious. You need company to get you home?"

"No, Tony is meeting me here at 5:30. But thanks for asking."

"Don't mention it. Let me know if there's anything you want me to do."

"Will do,"

At 5:30, Tony greeted Armand and stuck his head into Sarah's office. "You ready?"

She didn't say anything. She just got up and put her jacket on.

"Something wrong?"

She just shook her head took his arm and started walking toward past Armand's desk. "See you in the morning," she said to Armand and walked quietly to the elevator.

"What's up, Sarah?"

"I'm scared, Tony. I feel like I'm being hunted and I don't know by whom and from where it's coming."

When they got to her car in the garage, Tony noticed two men standing against a stanchion watching them. As they pulled out, "Did you recognize the men?" he asked.

"What men?"

"You didn't see the two guys standing back against the pole in the garage?"

"No, I didn't."

"Might have been nothing. They didn't bother us. But what the hell are they doing waiting in a garage?"

When they got to her building and pulled into her spot in the garage, she seemed to relax a little. "I'm really scared. I've never felt this way."

Tony smiled, "Nothing to worry about. Everything is under control."

They went to the lobby and Sarah took out her mail key. She took out the mail and scanned it. Nothing important, she thought. When they got to her apartment, she took off her coat and looked at the mail again. One envelope did not have an address, only her name. She opened it.

Sarah

We released you because we need your help. If you cooperate, everything will be fine and you will have nothing to worry about. If you don't, we cannot guarantee that you will survive the week.

We want Henry Stafford's password to the NSA website. You have until tomorrow noon to get it and text it to the following number. 202 555-3456. And be sure his access has not been discontinued. And do not alert the authorities.

"What's that?" Tony asked. She handed the note to him and looked at him while he was reading. "So now we know what they want? Can you get the password for them?"

"Probably."

"Then get it. Let me call Alberto first. Then I'll talk to Armitage and we'll figure a way to deal with it."

"But I'm in danger, aren't I?"

"I don't think so. Their threat is empty. If you don't cooperate, their deal will fail and they'll disappear to avoid getting caught. They only killed before to avoid discovery and keep their transaction intact. If the deal fails, there's no need."

"So why should I get the password for them?"

"Because we want to catch them. They are ruthless."

"I hope you're right, Tony. I really hope so," with an air of skepticism in her voice."

He called Alberto. "*Alberto, sono Tony.* Can you find the location of this cell number 202 555-3456?

"Hold on a minute," he answered. "It appears to be in the exact location as the Wintervale phone."

"Great. Thanks Alberto, *Ciao.*" He called Armitage. While it was ringing, he looked at her, "Just get the password and don't worry," He put the phone to his ear. "Bill, can we meet? I have more information for us. OK see you at the hotel bar in an hour."

"You're leaving me?"

"Just for a while. You're certainly not in danger now. They're counting on you. I want to work out a strategy to catch them." He looked at his watch. He kissed her nose. "Don't worry. I'll be back soon. Lock the door after me."

Sarah followed him to the door. "Soon." She locked the door, went back to the living room and turned on the TV.

Chapter XVII

May 25th Milan

"*Alberto, sono Muzzi.*"

"Ah. *Ciao, Maresciallo.* What's up?"

"Early this morning, a car pulled up at your building and a man was dropped off. He appeared to check the address, found the front door of the building locked and walked to the bar on the next block."

"Why would that bother you, *Maresciallo?*"

"The officer I assigned to your building last night, recognized the man."

"What did he look like?"

"He has a beard and he is known by our intelligence as a particularly vicious cyberspy. You obviously were correct in your suspicions."

"That's interesting. What do you think they are up to?"

"As you said, he must want something you have."

"Actually I don't have what he wants. But if he was sent by who I suspect he was, he may very well think I do."

"*Va bene.* Paolo is the day shift officer who just came on. He has been briefed and he is aware of the situation. I don't know if this culprit will try something by force during the day or wait until you leave sometime today or tonight. In any case, he has not been seen since this morning but we will stay alert."

"My wife is pregnant and fortunately she is in Como visiting her sister, so I don't have to worry her. I do suspect, though, that time is not something this guy has much of. I would guess he is very likely to try something as soon as he can."

Via Monti

The man with the beard suddenly appeared and was noticed by Paolo, who was stationed outside Alberto's apartment house. The man walked around the block and positioned himself at the electric gate to the garage area on the side street. He wanted to avoid going past the *portinaio*, who sat at a desk in the lobby screening visitors. Paolo waited at the front entrance unaware that the man was waiting at the garage gate. He called Alberto several times to warn him, but there was no answer.

After about five minutes, a car came up the ramp from the garage and remotely opened the gate. The man waited until the car was through and gone and just as the gate was almost closed, he slipped past it into the courtyard. He made his way to the service staircase and walked up to the second floor. He saw the letter B on the door and knocked.

Alberto didn't answer. The man knocked a second time with the same result. He took out a small kit and proceeded to pick the lock. Gun drawn, he opened the door and slid in quietly. He could hear the shower running. He tiptoed up to Alberto's computer, set his gun down and sat at the keyboard.

Armitage's office

When Tony met Bill Armitage, he presented the note Sarah received. Armitage read it. "You think they are serious?"

"Don't know."

"I have information for you. At your suggestion, we were tracking Flint's phone calls and found that he called a number in Milan, Italy yesterday. Do you think your Italian colleague is in some kind of danger?"

"It's possible. I have a good idea how they found out where he was. The tracking receipt when we sent the hard disk out. We always said that they might not have believed Sarah that the file was deleted. I think they have located Alberto and are making a simultaneous effort to find the file. I should really call him and give him a heads-up.. Armitage waited while Tony dialed Alberto." There was no answer. "Shit. Why doesn't he answer?" he mumbled. "I"ll try him again in a few minutes. What should we do regarding this threat to Sarah?" Tony asked.

"Well, she has to get Stafford's password. I know she can do that and I think she should. The question is what we do with it," Armitage answered, touching his nose, a habit when he was pondering something.

"The only reason we are going ahead is we want to catch these guys. If we fuck up their deal, they'll disappear and we won't know how serious they are about their threat to Sarah. I don't want to leave her in jeopardy like that."

Armitage said, "Agreed. We can probably locate that phone that she's supposed to text."

"I called Alberto a while ago. He said that phone is in the exact location of the Wintervale phone."

"How could they be so stupid? It's an anonymous phone. If I were doing it, I would keep the phone off and turn it on for a few seconds to get the password text and turn it off again. You'd never have time to locate it. What do we have on Flint? Do we know where he is?"

Armitage smiled. "Oh yeah. We've been tracking him for days now. He's in DC."

"Why don't we pick him up and question him. Maybe we can flip him. He's got to be worried about being charged with murder."

"I like that. We know Stafford was involved. There's this computer expert Theodore Wintervale, and Flint. Who else?"

"Apart from the flunkie muscle men, there's one more that I know of for sure, this guy that interrogated me with a hood on his head. He avoided being recognized at all costs. He disguised his voice. Flint must be able to identify him. I think from his behavior he must be the brains and the fact that he kept a hood on means he must be very recognizable. Maybe someone very high up. Your idea is a good one. We should pick up Flint. But let's wait until Sarah texts them the password. It will set wheels in motion and that's what we want."

"We can't let them succeed with the password. Obviously, they have this Wintervale guy who will probably be charged with obtaining the apps they are selling."

Tony answered, "We know where he is, right? Let's get to him and stop him from doing his job."

"OK, let's do it this way. We position FBI agents at Wintervale's and Flint's location. Flint is on the move so we have to follow him. It might be the same place, but we don't know that. Sarah texts the password right before noon. We pick up Flint. Then we pick up Wintervale. We keep them separate. Flint shouldn't know we've got Wintervale."

"Sounds perfect. Let me try Alberto again. No answer," he said. "That worries me because he's very responsive. Talk to you later."

Milan

Alberto turned off the shower, dried himself off and walked into his bedroom to get dressed. He was not aware that the computer in his office was being used. Ten minutes later, he walked into his office facing the bearded man with a gun pointed at him. "Who are you? How did you get in here?"

"Sit down and be quiet," the bearded man said. "Who I am is none of your business. What I want is within your capability."

"And just what is that?" he said.

"I want the NSA file in the Amerada account?"

Alberto laughed. "Can't help you. It's been erased. Sorry."

"Try again. Why would you erase it?"

"The people to whom it belongs, don't need that file. They own the apps. Out there only makes the file available to an entity that shouldn't have it."

"I don't believe you." the bearded man said, cocking his pistol. "I would have no qualms about blowing you away. If you really don't have it, you are not needed. Last chance." Alberto laughed raucously. The man said sarcastically," You think this is funny?"

"Very funny. Tell me, what is your name?" Before the man could answer, Alberto's cell phone rang. "May I answer that?"

"Sure. But say something you shouldn't and I will blow your head off."

"*Pronto*, DeSanctis here."

"Ah Tony." He listened, then glanced at the bearded man. "I already have the visitor. He's holding a gun on me. I'm in no danger. He wants the file but I told him it's been erased."

"Get off the phone," the man said.

"Sure." Alberto smiled again. "Talk to you later, Tony." and disconnected.

"You are either incredibly courageous or just plain stupid."

"Neither," Alberto watched the bearded man's body crumple to the floor as Paolo, the carabiniere officer who had surreptitiously come into the apartment, hit him over the head with the butt of his gun. Alberto winced at the sound. "*Grazie, Paolo.*"

"*Niente,* Alberto." He called Muzzi to send someone over to get the man. "*Il Maresciallo vuol parlarti?*" he said, handing Alberto his phone.

"*Si, Maresciallo.* I'm fine. Paolo arrived in time. *Grazie.* I knew I could count on you." He gave the phone back to Paolo, took his own phone and called Tony. "*Ciao, amico mio.* Yes, everything is OK. A bearded man broke into my apartment and at gunpoint, wanted the file. The carabiniere officer who has been watching over me for a week now, saw and recognized the guy, sneaked into my apartment and hit him with his gun while he was threatening me. No damage done. What's happening on your end?"

Tony explained the threat to Sarah and what they were planning. "Sarah is frightened," Tony added. "She wants this spy stuff over and get back to her desk job."

Alberto laughed. "Tell her to enjoy the challenge and the excitement. I'll bet she will never be happy in a bureaucratic job any longer."

"I'll tell her what you said. But I doubt she'll believe it, at least not now. I'll keep you posted. Glad you're OK. You worried me for a while not answering your phone."

"I was in the shower. I'm allowed," he added.

"No excuse. Get yourself a waterproof phone."

"Bye, Tony. Best to Sarah." Alberto hung up just at the carabiniere arrived and the bearded man started to come to. "Who sent you?" Alberto asked.

The bearded man felt his head where he was hit, looked at Alberto and said nothing.

"You're going to wind up in San Vittore prison. The only question is how long you want to stay there. Help me and I'll help you."

After a few seconds of thought, "A man named Herman Flint, from America. I was recommended to him."

"By whom?" Alberto asked.

"He didn't say and I don't know. Any one of a number of people. I have a reputation, you know."

"I know. The carabinieri told me who you were. OK, it's your problem, now. Good luck."

"Wait. I really don't know who recommended me. I got a call from this guy Flint. He offered me 5,000 euros to get this file from your computer. That's all I know."

"Paolo, if he gets a phone call, don't let him answer it. And don't let him make one. We don't want this Flint to know whether he succeeded or not. Now you should take him. He's no help. And thanks again for saving me. That's two I owe you. I haven't forgotten the Moffett case."

Paolo laughed. "Always glad to help. You enjoy the challenges. So do I. *Ciao*, Alberto."

Armitage's office

Bill Armitage called Andy Noble to arrange what he and Tony had decided to do. "Andy, I think you should have agents at the two locations as soon as you can get them there. Wintervale is probably nailed to where he is because that's where his computer is. Flint's location is another story because he may be on the move. So get to his location right away and keep tabs on his movements. If he's not there call me right away. When you get my text message, which I will send after they get the password, pick up Flint and Wintervale. But with Wintervale make sure he acknowledges to someone he has received the password."

"How do you know he'll do that?" Andy asked.

"There was an ultimatum issued to Sarah. He would want to know if she did what he demanded with his threat."

"What if he doesn't call?"

"Just stop him from doing anything on the computer and wait. I'm sure he will be contacted. The objective is to stop him from using the password he received other than checking to see if it works and to make sure his boss, whoever that is, knows he got the password."

"I get the idea. OK we'll get on it right now."

"Keep me posted if there are any unanticipated movements."

"Gotcha. We'll talk later."

Sarah's office

Sarah sat nervously at her desk waiting for time to pass. Armand stuck his head in. "I'm going to order lunch in. You wan't anything?"

"No, thanks." She forced a smile. "I'm going out as soon as I take care of some details."

"OK. Let me know if you change your mind." She shook her head and looked at her watch. Only a half hour to wait, she thought. Then she had to watch out. She knew as soon as she gave out the password, she would be a target because Stafford's account will be disabled a half hour after she released the password. She got up and went to the window to look down at the street. There wasn't much to see from her high up window except the tops of cars but it was something to pass time and calm her down.

Theodore

Theodore's cell phone rang. "Answer it," the agent said. Theodore was flustered and frightened.

"What should I say?" he asked.

The agent responded, "Tell him the password worked but you haven't got the files yet. That will take awhile. Don't say anything else. Keep in mind you're looking at murder charges, so it's in your interest to behave."

Theodore answered his phone. "Yes, she texted the password. It worked, Mr. Flint. But it will take time for me to find and download the files. Yes, as soon as I can."

The agent took Theodore's phone from him and hit the off button. "Now pack up your computer. Do you have a box or something to put it in?"

Theodore shook his head and pulled out a black nylon bag. He started dismantling the peripheral components and put the computer in the bag with the peripheral hard drives. The agent cuffed him and the other agent took the black bag. "Andy, this is Phil. We got Wintervale and his computer. Everything went as planned here. We're bringing him in. OK see you soon."

FBI offices

Right after his call to Theodore, Flint was picked up by two FBI agents. He was now sitting in an interrogation room with Andy Noble and Bill Armitage. "Why am I here?" he asked.

Armitage said, "You are being charged with, among other things, theft of government property, possibly murder, and certainly kidnapping."

"I don't know what you are talking about."

Armitage laughed, "Who are your cohorts? You don't want to suffer this alone, do you?"

"You have no proof of anything. I want a lawyer. Let me call my lawyer."

"No need for the moment. We won't ask you any questions."

They waited for several minutes without saying anything. Then, Tony barged into the room and sat down. Flint's mouth fell open in shock. "Remember me?" Tony said, smiling directly at Flint.

"No," Flint said, obviously lying, but what choice did he have?

"Suit yourself. Tony responded."

"Yes, I know who you are. I didn't recognize you at first," he lied again.

Looking at Armitage, Tony asked, "Did anyone read him his rights?"

"Yes, the agent did when he brought him in," Armitage responded.

"Who was the hooded man that interrogated me?" Tony asked.

"I don't know," Flint said, calmly. "I really don't. He kept himself hooded from me as well. I only know him as Galahad, nothing else."

"Is he the leader of your little cabal?"

Flint hesitated. "I really don't know. I know he's the one that gave me my instructions and will eventually be the one who cuts me in for my share."

"You can forget about that," Armitage smiled. "You're going away for a long time. How long depends on how much you cooperate."

"I don't know who he is. And I had nothing to do with the murders or your kidnapping."

"That's hard to believe. How much were you selling the files for?"

"I'm not sure. I think 300 million dollars."

"How much were you getting?"

"20 million."

"And you trusted a man you didn't know to pay you 20 million dollars to get involved in murder and kidnapping?"

Tony interrupted. "No matter. We'll get him with or without your help. It's all the same to us. But it would matter significantly to you if you help."

Armitage asked, "Who was your customer?"

"I don't know. Just that it was a Russian."

"You don't know his name?"

"No."

"How about Theodore Wintervale? You know him?"

"Yes, he's the computer expert. He did the killing,"

"I see," Tony said. "You had nothing to do with the killings. Hard to believe."

"When I found out about them, I was very concerned."

Tony asked, "Why didn't you call the police? You must know that you are now an accessory."

"He would have had me killed," Flint answered.

"Who?" Armitage asked.

"Galahad."

"What did he plan for me?" Tony asked.

"He didn't say. But I suspect he would have eliminated you as well. Especially since you could identify me, and eventually find out who he is."

Andy asked, "What do you know about him? Where does he live?"

"I have no idea," Flint answered.

"How does he get in touch with you?"

"Cell phone. I want to call my lawyer."

Andy looked at Armitage. "Where's his phone?"

"It's being analyzed. I should get some significant information before the day is over. Andy, you've got enough to hold him, don't you?"

"Oh, yeah."

Armitage pronounced, "Let him call his lawyer then lock him up. I'll keep you posted on the results of the phone analysis." Tony and Bill Armitage left the room. Armitage said to Tony. "What do you think will happen next?"

"Don't know. I don't think they'll give up so easily. I don't know if this Galahad is the top dog or just a cog in a big wheel."

"That worries me about Sarah. She's the only link they have to the files. There's too much money at stake for them to stop. They've killed before and would have no qualms about doing so again. In fact, I would be careful myself if I were you." Tony looked surprised. "They must know about your relationship to Sarah and that without you around she's much more vulnerable. And I'm sure they already know that Wintervale doesn't have the files."

"Maybe not. If we're lucky, he hasn't been made yet. He did acknowledge that he had the password, it worked but he didn't yet have the files. Let's go see him." Tony suggested.

They went up one flight to an identical interrogation room where two agents were talking to Wintervale. Before they went in, they continued watching through the one-way glass. Theodore Wintervale was obviously very frightened. He didn't know what to expect.

Sarah's office

Sarah got up from desk, put her coat on and walked past Armand. "Going to lunch?" he asked.

"Yes," she said unconvincingly.

"When will you be back?" he asked. "Just want to know what to tell callers."

"Not sure. I'm meeting someone for lunch. See you later."

Armand's eyes followed Sarah down the corridor to the elevator as if trying to figure out what was on Sarah's plate. Her behavior was strange and he did not know what to make of it.

Sarah was depressed. Her life was suddenly out of her control. She couldn't enjoy the new found interest she had in Tony. The routine of her job and her life had changed. She didn't know if she was in any danger. It was becoming too much for her. She called Tony to ask what was happening.

Tony tried to summarize everything in one lump. "We stopped the sale of the file, for sure. We have the two in custody. So far, nothing has been discovered by this guy Galahad who seems to be running things."

"What happens now?"

"Not sure. We are trying to find Galahad but it is not easy. He is very shrewd and very private."

"What will happen when he finds out he's been screwed?" she said with a nasty tone.

"Don't know yet. We're hoping he does something that gives us a lead to him."

"That doesn't make me feel too good."

Tony, sensing her mood asked, "Sarah, what's wrong?"

"Everything," she said. "Everything," she repeated. "I'm just not used to this kind of continuous tension."

"Come over to the FBI building. I'm on the third floor. Did you have lunch?"

"Not hungry, but I'll be there in about fifteen."

Galahad

Galahad realized something was wrong. He would have heard something from Flint by now. He waited another hour then called Yuri after he got no answer from either Flint or Theodore. "I am not confident we can complete the transaction. Something is wrong."

"What?" he asked.

"I don't know. I no longer use my old phone. This is my new number. Tell me where to transfer your payment. I will refund it immediately."

"That does not make me very happy. I will lose a very large commission,"

"I can imagine. But I will lose much more as well, unless I can figure a way to restore the situation."

"If you think you can, I can try to hold off on a cancellation."

"I am certainly willing to make the effort, but at this point I am not very optimistic. I have to be honest with you."

"How much time do you think you need?"

Galahad thought for a moment. His mind was beginning to plot again. "Give me a month. I will do nothing for two weeks to relieve the police pressure and then see if I can set wheels in motion to obtain the merchandise."

"I think I can give you that. It's certainly worth a try if you are willing."

"We are agreed, then. What should I do with the money?"

"I am an optimist," Yuri answered. "Hold it for the month. Meanwhile, the interest on the money can provide expense money for you."

"Thanks. I will be in touch. Don't call me. This phone is being taken out of commission." Galahad took a padded envelope out of his drawer. He carefully erased his contacts from his anonymous phone, removed the SIM chip and broke it into four pieces. He checked to make sure the phone was fully charged. He addressed the padded envelope, left his phone on, and put it in. He sealed the envelope, picked up the pieces of the chip and went directly to the post office. As soon as he got outside, he scattered the pieces of the chip.

Armitage's office

Herman Flint and Theodore Wintervale were both being held incommunicado and separately. Two days had passed but they had not been charged yet. Andy Noble had prepared the information for the justice department to file charges against them, recommending that they be held without bail for a period of time to prevent any communication with Galahad.

Bill Armitage called his forensic office. "Nothing?"

"When we finally located the phone yesterday, it was in the DC post office right downtown."

"Where is it now?"

"I cannot locate it. I would guess it's on an airplane."

"Great," Armitage spoke sarcastically. Galahad has probably skipped out, he thought. Now they would never find him. He called Tony, who was at Sarah's office. "The phone is not locatable. My guy thinks it must be on an airplane. It was at the post office yesterday. He was probably mailing something. Now he's gone."

"You seem in better spirits, today, Sarah,"Armand said.

Tony answered, "Things seem to be settling back to normal. We've got the bad guys."

"That's great. Was it some kind of evil ring?"

"Not that dramatic, Armand. You watch too much TV," Sarah interjected.

"Can you tell me what it was all about? Or is it still too classified?" he asked. "I've been curious, since you were assaulted in the garage. You haven't been your usual stoic self, Sarah."

She laughed. "I'll tell you all about it. But not now. I've got too much catching up to do. That is, with my normal bureaucratic shit."

Tony looked at his watch. "I gotta go, Sarah. Are you giving me a lift to the airport?"

"You bet. Let's go."

"Nice meeting you, Tony."

"Same here, Armand." They shook hands and Tony left with Sarah. During the ride to National Airport, Alberto called Tony asking for a status situation.

"Hey, we stopped the sale, got the bad guys. But we think the *pezzo di novanta* got away. We don't know."

Alberto said, "Did you know the phone with the number you gave me is now in the American Embassy in Moscow?"

"Big cheese, an American diplomat? Doesn't make any sense."

"Why don't you call it?"

Sarah took out her anonymous phone, "Here, Tony, try it on this."

"What's the number?"

He keyed it in as Alberto dictated. "Message, not available."

"If the SIM card was removed, you have to be on the same WiFi network. That's why I couldn't call." Alberto said. "Try them one at a time."

"I'll do that and call you back." Tony went through each of the providers: AT&T, Sprint, T-Mobile then finally the call went through.

"Hello," came the reply.

"Who is this?" Tony asked.

"Who are you?" the female voice asked.

"Tony Belvedere, New York Police Department.

"This is Millie Dawes, assistant consular officer in the American Embassy in Moscow."

"Is that your phone?"

"No."

"Whose is it?"

"I have no idea. It just came in the mail, addressed to no one in the embassy"

"May I ask you to send it to Sarah Tepper at NSA in Washington. Send the package it came in as well. You should have the address."

"It came in a padded envelope. Whose phone is it, anyway?"

"Don't know. But it's evidence in a murder case. Will you send it?"

"Certainly. Give me her name again. Got it. It will go out in a diplomatic mail pouch then mailed from DC. OK?"

"Great. Thanks, Millie." He looked at Sarah. "Looks like the phone skipped. The big cheese didn't."

"Shit. Does that mean I'm still in danger?"

"I can't see why. Whoever he is, revenge is not his objective. Money is. And he doesn't want to get caught. He must know by now that Flint and Wintervale are being held. My guess he has two choices. Disappear or ..."

"Or what?" she asked glancing into his eyes.

"Or try again after waiting for things to cool."

"He's coming after me again?"

"Not likely. It turned out very badly the first time. I think he has to find another source." He pulled up to the departure entrance. "Don't worry." he kissed her cheek gently, then her mouth. "I'll call you when I get home."

CHAPTER XVIII

June 2nd

Things had calmed down dramatically. Bill Armitage had all but given up on finding Galahad. They had nothing that would give them any lead as to who or where he was. They assumed he was the head man. They had no information or evidence that he was working for someone else, especially since he had dropped from the radar. Both Flint and Wintervale were no help in finding him because he had kept himself isolated and his identity concealed. The only time Flint was anywhere near him was when they kidnapped Tony and he was hooded. The only thing he could say was he was about five foot ten and slim

The cell phone came back from the Moscow Embassy and the forensics people, first at NSA and then in Tony's department in New York couldn't find anything. Tony thought about sending the phone to Alberto but decided that even the Milanese genius wouldn't be able to uncover anything.

Both Armitage and Tony were uncomfortable and felt that this caper wasn't over yet. But Tony wouldn't let on to Sarah how he felt. Sarah was too strung out about it. Tony felt she was tough enough to handle it.

The Amerada account was left intact. They all felt that its presence might just provoke a return to the scene of the crime. But so far, nothing. Alberto could trace nothing either but he became obsessed with the Moscow connection. Somehow he felt that if he could locate the buyer, it would eventually lead him to the seller, that is, Galahad. So he continued pushing his research.

Yuri had not heard anything yet from Galahad. He could not call him because he did not have his new number. He went to see Valery who was still in rehab and awaiting another surgery to repair his maimed face. He was optimistic that Galahad would eventually succeed. He didn't know why he felt that way, but it kept him thinking positively.

Sarah was leaving her apartment and stopped to get her mail on the way down to the garage. There was only a small greeting card size envelope. She opened it and read the carefully hand-lettered text:

Sarah:

I want you to set up the following account at NSA. User name is Galahad. Password is 363636#. Tell no one about this, I repeat, no one. I will not contact you again. If it is not done by noon today, your future will be very short.

Sarah started to shake as she hurried to her car. When she got into the car, she took out her anonymous phone and started to call Bill Armitage but stopped herself. Tell no one, it said. She had to think about it. She rushed to her office and right past Armand, who, when his "Good Morning" was ignored, followed her to her office. "Something wrong, Sarah?" he said, sticking his head into her office.

"Something personal, Armand. Nothing that would interest you."

"Let me know if there's something I can do."

"Nothing, thanks. Close the door please." Sarah sat staring at the wall for at least fifteen minutes. She answered her ringing office phone. "Tepper," she said.

"Sarah, Bill. Armand called me. He was worried about you. You OK?"

"Yeah, I'm OK. Just a little down."

"OK. Call me if you need me." He called Tony in New York."Tony, Sarah's got me worried. Maybe you can find out what's bothering her."

"What happened?"

"Armand called me a little while ago and said she ignored his greeting and went into her office. He said she always says good morning no matter what."

"Don't you think it's a little overreaction? Maybe she's just let down from the conclusion of the Amerada thing."

"Maybe," he said. "Just the same I would like you to call her and call me back with your reaction."

Alberto called Tony. "Tony. I was thinking about the possibility of flushing this Galahad out. We can't just leave him alone. That means he's controlling things. If there's one thing I've learned, it's to try to control events. It forces the target into mistakes. If we leave him alone, there's nothing to put a monkey-wrench into his plans. That's how they say it, no? By the way, what is a monkey wrench?"

Tony laughed. "Yeah, that's one way to say it. A monkey wrench? *Una chiave Inglese, grande.* But tell me, what did you have in mind?"

"I have been trying to get information about the Moscow guy with no result. But I know his email address. Suppose I try to create the impression that there is another seller of the same apps."

Tony smiled instinctively. "That's certainly worth trying. What return email address will you use?"

"I have one I can use. It's almost impossible to trace."

"Do it, then. Call me when you get something. If there's interest, I'll call him. *Ciao.*" Tony called Sarah. "Bill is worried about you."

"Why is that?" Sarah responded trying to sound nonchalant.

"Armand called Bill, said he was concerned that you're not yourself. Something's wrong. What is it?"

"Nothing. I'm just a little down."

"Bullshit, Sarah. What's up?" he insisted.

Sarah fought back tears. She was scared and didn't know what to do. "Tony, I got a threat."

"Really, what kind of threat?"

"A note in my mailbox this morning."

"Read it to me." he demanded. Sarah took it out of her purse, and read it slowly. Tony responded instantly. "Idle threat. It's a bluff."

"Are you sure?"

"Very. Call Bill and bring it over to his office so he can look at it. Maybe there's something he can spot."

"What should I do about the account?"

"Set up the account just before noon with password just as he demanded. Give it about a half hour and cancel the password. Can you do that?"

"Sure. But why?"

"Whoever it is will try at noon. If it works, he will think he's got it. But you and I both know it will take hours to find the files and then download them. And that's assuming he has nothing else to do, has the technical facility to do it or has to get someone else. A half hour does him no good. Maybe it will cause him to expose himself somehow."

Sarah laughed a forced laugh, "Not literally, I hope."

"Funny, funny. I'll call Alberto and tell him what's going on. Meanwhile, take the note to Bill and tell him the same thing."

"I'm really afraid, Tony."

"Nothing to be afraid of. Chill. He's lost without you. And if you refuse this time, he's got to try again. He can't hurt you."

"Should I alert Armand? As sort of protection?"

"For the moment, the fewer people who know, the better. Tell him about the threat, sure. But don't tell him what you're doing."

"Going out, Sarah?" Armand asked.

"Yeah. Got some things to do. Just so you know, I got a threatening note this morning. I'm not supposed to tell anyone but I'm scared, so keep an eye out."

"I will certainly do that. Something you have to do?"

"Yes. But don't ask any more. I don't want you to get into any kind of trouble. Just watch my back."

"You got it." he said, smiling.

Later

"Yuri, I think I may be able to salvage our deal after all."

"Galahad? I'm very glad you called. I've been frustrated not being able to call you. I got an anonymous email saying that the files I want are available and do I want to make a bid. You have any idea who it is?"

"I can't imagine," Galahad answered. "That worries me. I have no idea what's going on. I know of another customer as you well know but I had no idea someone else is soliciting you as a buyer."

Yuri answered, "Do you think they're also going after the other buyer, just as you did?"

"I would have to assume so. All I can say is it must be someone that knows what has happened and someone who has access. And I no longer have Theodore to explore the cyber activity. I'll see what I can find out and get back to you. Meanwhile, I am working on procuring the files."

"Goodbye," Yuri abruptly disconnected.

Armitage's office

Bill Armitage read the note and scrutinized the card it was written on. He looked at the lettering. "Not easy to identify anyone from lettering, particularly when it's done slowly and carefully. It's the shortcuts that give the handwriting its distinctive character. This note carefully avoids any."

"Tony says I have nothing to worry about. He has no other source without me."

"He's right, Sarah. Without you, Galahad is lost. The only thing I would watch out for is another attempt to frighten you. Always keep in the back of your mind that he will not kill you. He might physically hurt you if he could get access with your help."

"Suppose he kidnaps me again?"

Bill frowned. "If that happens, do what he wants. We don't want you to get hurt. Just do it slowly and make mistakes because you are nervous and not used to this stuff. But anything you do on the computer can and will be tracked by us and your Italian friend."

"And when I succeed? What'll he do then? I'm no dope, Bill. Once he gets what he wants, I'm a dead woman."

Armitage thought for a minute. "You can't be hurt until he closes his deal. He knows it failed before. So he has to make sure it works." He stood up suddenly. "Can you give Alberto access? To upload files?"

"That's easy. I can't give him access to download anything or read anything. That would be a no-no."

Bill picked up his phone. "Tony, I want you to do something for us."

Sarah's office

Sarah looked at her watch when she returned to her office. She still had almost an hour to set up the account for Galahad, planning to do so at the last minute. Armand poked his head in. "I have a noon appointment for lunch. Anything you want me to do before I leave?"

"Can't think of anything. Got a date?"

"I wish," he said. "Just meeting an old college chum. To catch up."

"Have fun," she said. She called Tony. "Hello, my love." she said casually.

"You sound better. You still scared?"

"Absolutely terrified, but fatalistic."

He laughed. "I'm coming down tonight. Got room for me to stay?"

"I can put a folding chair in the kitchen. Or the bathroom if you prefer. But only if you take me out to dinner."

"Deal. Wanna pick me up at the airport? Gets in at 5:40."

"Will do. See you then."

At five minutes before noon, Sarah set up the account as was demanded and then called the Chinese take-out kitchen for a hot and sour soup and chicken with garlic sauce. She didn't want to get distracted until she had cancelled the access according to the plan. At promptly 12:30 her lunch order arrived. She paid the delivery man with a generous tip and before she opened the containers, she cancelled Galahad's password. She was still eating and reading a newspaper when Armand returned and stuck his head in to her office. "Everything copacetic?"

"So far. I'm still here."

He laughed. "Anyway, I'm back."

For the next several hours, Sarah buried herself in paperwork. The Amerada thing had set her behind. She was meticulous about records and so hated doing the obligatory data management that she never let it build up. But now, she had to catch up and restore her routine. At 4:30, she locked her desk and left to get Tony at National Airport.

Tony's plane was a few minutes late getting to the gate. Getting off the plane, he walked to the waiting room and scanned it for Sarah and saw only several drivers holding up cards. He walked outside and looked for her car. She must have hit traffic, he thought. He called her cell phone which went to the anonymous message she put on it. That made him worry. He called Bill Armitage. "Bill, Tony. Sarah was supposed to pick me up at the airport but didn't show. Have you seen her?"

"I talked to her early this afternoon right after she cancelled the password she set up. I haven't seen or spoken to her since then."

"I'm concerned. It's not like her."

"Not to worry. Hop a cab. I'll meet you at her apartment." Bill called Sarah's office extension. No answer. Armand must have left already. He drove to Sarah's apartment and just as he pulled up Tony was getting out of an Uber car. As they shook hands, Bill said, "I checked her office. Nothing. Armand had already left. You don't happen to have Armand's cell phone number, do you?"

"No. I never had occasion to call him and he never called me," Tony said, as they got on the elevator. Tony opened the door of her apartment with the key Sarah gave him. They looked around. "I don't think she came home. She must have left the office to come get me directly." Tony tried her phone again. Message, again.

Tony phoned Alberto. "Alberto, Sarah *si e' scomparsa*. Can you track her? I have been trying to follow but her phone is off."

"I did put the fake files on the system for her, so she can safely download them. Where did you lose her?"

"It was in her office building, somewhere."

"They probably waylaid her in the garage. I didn't think it would be so soon. Can you keep an eye out?"

"Sure. When she accesses the files, I'm pretty sure I can locate her."

"Keep me posted, *Ciao*."

Armitage called Andy Noble. "Andy, Sarah's missing. We think she was snatched when she went to her car."

"I know."

"You know? How?"

"I sent two agents to keep watch around quitting time. They got there just in time to see Sarah being pushed into a black Ford sedan. They followed her to a warehouse in Bethesda. I was just going to call you."

"You're amazing. Can you text me the address?"

"Sure. My guys are waiting for my instructions. They won't do anything until I say so."

"Tell them to sit tight. We'll be there in about a half hour. Traffic won't be great right now."

"Will do, my friend. Take care." Andy answered.

"Let's go, Tony."

Sarah captive again

Sarah had her hood removed and saw that she was sitting in front of a notebook computer. "We want you to reactivate the password you cancelled," one of the men said. When she looked up, he turned her head back. "If you value your life, you will not turn around. If you recognize any of us, you will leave us no choice."

"OK," she repeated, "OK."

The two men who kidnapped her were standing behind her. Between them was a third man who said nothing. Sarah did not know how many were standing behind her but assumed that this Galahad was present, but not speaking. Someone she knew or would recognize. The man who gave her the instructions was the man that pushed her into the car and said 'let's go' to the driver.

"It's done." One of the men put a hood over her head immediately.

"A word of warning. You tricked me before," whispered one of the men. "If you've done it again, you are a dead woman. Do I make myself clear?"

"Yes, It was done."

"Last chance. If you've tricked me, fix it now."

"No trick. The password is valid and I'll leave it valid," she added, calmly.

"Hands behind your back," one of the men said. He cuffed her hands together with a plastic strip. One of the men waved to the other two and pointed to a back door. Leaving Sarah hooded and cuffed, they left.

Sarah sat quietly, thinking about who she knew that could do such a thing. Someone at NSA but who? Stafford was dead. Her boss? She couldn't believe he was smart enough. The only other person was Bill Armitage. He couldn't have fooled both her and

Tony. Who? Who? She asked herself over and over. She knew many people at NSA.

Suddenly, she heard the door being broken open and people entering. "Sarah, you OK?" said Tony's voice, pulling the hood off her head. "You got a knife?" he asked Bill, who handed him a opened pocket knife. When her hands were freed, she stood up and grabbed Tony. "I see the back door open. When did they leave?"

"About ten minutes ago," she answered.

"Damn," Bill said. "My bad, they shouldn't have waited for us."

"Sarah, do you know who it was?" Tony asked.

"There were the two who grabbed me and finally a third man whispered a warning at me not to trick him again."

"Must be the same guy that whispered when they grabbed me," Tony said.

"How did you find me?"

"You can thank Andy Noble who anticipated this and followed the men who snatched you. Too bad, we missed them," Armitage said.

"Let's go back to my apartment," Sarah said. "I would like a tumbler full of scotch." They all agreed. Bill called Andy to give him an update on the situation.

During the trip to her apartment, Sarah said nothing. "What's up, Sarah?" Tony asked.

"I keep asking myself who could it be. I keep drawing blanks. It has to be someone who has not been involved and is off my radar screen. I'm not so oblivious that if it were someone close, I would know by now."

Milan

Interesting, Alberto thought. He didn't know the players so photos wouldn't help him. He looked at the photo in front of him. He had succeeded in hacking into the computer Sarah was at, as she was using it and activated the camera on the screen. He could see the woman whom he assumed was Sarah and three men standing behind her. He had recorded several images and at least one of them was at the proper angle and had the faces very clear.

He called Tony. "*Ciao*, my friend. How is Sarah?"

"She's fine, Alberto. But we missed the kidnappers and the *pezzo di novanta* who got away. They also took the notebook computer she was using. She was not able to turn to look at them so we still don't know who he is."

"I just may be able to help," Alberto said.

"How," Tony asked.

"I will text you a photo I took from the computer Sarah was using."

"How did you do that?"

"I am a genius, you know," Alberto said.

"*Dai, Alberto, dimmi tutto*. Tell me everything."

I hacked into the computer and activated the photo app on the computer. One photo in particular of Sarah and the men behind her is clear as a bell. I will text it to you right now."

The three watched the screen on Tony's telephone until the message appeared. Tony hit the photo to enlarge it and the three of them said the name, simultaneously. "Armand."

CHAPTER XIX

June 3

Armand was surprised when two FBI agents knocked on his door. "Armand Arnaud?"

"Yes," he said to the two men he saw after opening the door.

"Agent Villanova of the FBI. You are under arrest. Please put your hands behind your back."

"What is this all about? This must be a mistake."

"Turn around please. We'll sort it out at our offices."

He went quietly and when he got to FBI offices, he was told it was in his interest to cooperate with them otherwise he risked years in prison. They didn't mentions the murders he was obviously responsible for. He did as he was instructed by the FBI agents and called Yuri.

"Yuri, I can provide the merchandise but I am reluctant to do it by email. I am afraid my email has been compromised."

"What do you suggest?" Yuri asked.

"We should meet somewhere and I can give it to you directly."

"Where?"

"Why don't you come to Washington. Take your time so that things can cool down. You pick a day."

Yuri was apprehensive. "That sounds very risky."

"Why don't you suggest something. I'm amenable to any suggestion except coming to Moscow."

Yuri laughed. "I can see why. All right, I'll come to Washington in three days. I'll call you then. Fortunately, I have diplomatic immunity. The last thing I need is to be arrested by your FBI,"

"Let me know your flight number and I'll meet you at the airport. It's safer that way."

"Is this the phone you want me to call?" Yuri asked.

"No need to call. Just text the flight number with no other information."

"Fine. See you then."

June 6th

Sarah sat at her desk with Tony opposite her. "Well," she said, things are very anti-climactic."

"Are you upset about it?" he laughed. "I was told you would never be the same again. You would no longer be content with being a bureaucrat." Before she answered, the phone rang.

"Hi Andy. What's up?" Sarah answered, "Really. That's great, thanks for the info."

"This Russian, Yuri Malenkov was arrested by the FBI. They couldn't hold him because of his diplomatic status, but the state department banned him from entering the U.S. in the future. This also guarantees that his phone will be under surveillance forever."

"That's great. So things are over?"

"Except for Armand who will probably be charged with murder and I'll have to testify unless he plea bargains. Despite what you've heard, I long for the peaceful bureaucratic days. Tell me, my sweet, how long can we keep up this long range relationship, especially since the case that brought us together is over?"

"It does present difficulties but it is said that we Italians, *si arrangiano*."

"What does that mean?"

"It means we arrange things." he answered. She came around from her desk and grabbed him, looked him in the eyes, "I love you," she kissed him intensely.

THE END

About The Author

Alan Wallach was born and raised in Brooklyn. He has a degree in chemistry from Brooklyn College After a tour in the US Air Force as a meteorologist, he went to work for IBM and back to school for graduate study in mathematics at NYU. He has been associated with computers for most of his business life in one form or another. For almost 15 years wrote a computer column for the Sunday Berkshire Eagle in Pittsfield MA. In the early nineties, his Plain English Guide to Your PC was published and and right before the millennium, The Year 2000 Hoax was released, a book which debunked the doomsayers prediction of an economic collapse because of the Y2K bug.

Alan is an accomplished classical pianist and considers music his first love. He is a basketball nut and still plays often in the early morning hours with a similar minded group of nuts.

He and his wife have recently moved from the Berkshires in Massachusetts to the New York City area He is now working on a new novel and his Kieran series of books for young readers.

You can read his rants on his blog at

www.alanwallach.com/blog.